Elizabeth. His family's kitchen maid!

An American in the outskirts of London. A girl with dough under her nails and tomato-sauce stains on her uniform. A girl whose warmth and compassion and kindness radiated from her sweet face.

A girl who Max couldn't stop thinking about.

It was ironic. At Max's side sat the girl who history, family, and—if you believed his father—*destiny* had provided for him. Max flicked his eyes at his fiancée. With her swanlike neck and porcelain complexion, Lavinia was inarguably beautiful. She was also, Max knew very well, cultured, intelligent, witty, and—by any measure—a good catch.

But she left him cold.

You've got to face the fact that you've got a monster crush on the scullery maid, mate, Max thought, restraining himself from groaning aloud. As much as he wanted to pretend it wasn't happening, the fact was that his affections—and admiration—for Elizabeth were only growing by the day.

And so was the countdown to his wedding.

Bantam Books in the Elizabeth series.
Ask your bookseller for the books you have missed.

#1 University, Interrupted
#2 London Calling
#3 A Royal Pain

Elizabeth

A Royal Pain

WRITTEN BY
LAURIE JOHN

CREATED BY
FRANCINE PASCAL

BANTAM BOOKS
NEW YORK · TORONTO · LONDON · SYDNEY · AUCKLAND

RL: 8, AGES 014 AND UP

A ROYAL PAIN
A Bantam Book / March 2001

Sweet Valley High® and Sweet Valley University®
are registered trademarks of Francine Pascal.
Elizabeth is a trademark owned by Francine Pascal.
Conceived by Francine Pascal.

Produced by 17th Street Productions,
an Alloy Online, Inc. company.
33 West 17th Street
New York, NY 10011.

ISBN: 0-553-49355-8

Visit us on the Web! www.randomhouse.com/teens

Published simultaneously in the United States and Canada

Bantam Books is an imprint of Random House Children's Books, a division
of Random House, Inc. BANTAM BOOKS and the rooster colophon are
registered trademarks of Random House, Inc. Bantam Books, 1540
Broadway, New York, New York 10036.

PRINTED IN THE UNITED STATES OF AMERICA

OPM   0 9 8 7 6 5 4 3 2 1

To Alice Elizabeth Wenk

Chapter One

"Trying to get me fat before the wedding?"

Pardon? Max Pennington thought as his fiancée, Lavinia Thurston, turned her cool blue eyes on him like he was crazy. All he'd done was ask her if she wanted more crisps.

"Max, that's the eight-hundredth time you've asked me if I wanted more crisps, and the answer is still *no*." Lavinia shook her head slowly. "You know I'm dieting." She poked a finger in Max's rock-hard abs, then settled down into his side to watch the flickering screen.

Max sighed and stuffed a handful of crisps into his mouth. Crumbs scattered over his broadcloth shirt and jeans. The truth was, Max kept asking Lavinia the same question because he was worried that if he stopped paying "attention" to her, she would immediately guess the real subject he couldn't get off his

1

mind for even one second: his family's new kitchen maid, Elizabeth Bennet.

As usual, he and Lavinia were hanging out at her estate, watching a video as they always did on Thursdays. For the past month he'd had to suffer through wedding videos, documentaries on furnishing your first home and the like. Ugh. So tonight he'd taken charge of the video renting and brought over a bunch of American action flicks starring Bruce Willis. Although truth be told, he would have preferred to rewatch the entire BBC *Pride and Prejudice* video set than sit through another explosion reflecting off Willis's bald spot.

Pride and Prejudice . . . featuring, of course, the ineluctable Elizabeth Bennet. Somehow, even in the presence of his supposedly beloved fiancée, everything seemed to lead Max's thoughts back to Elizabeth Bennet tonight.

Max tried to keep his mind on Bruce Willis and the aliens he was taking out with a gun that looked more like a small helicopter, but it was hopeless. Lavinia looked absolutely miserable at his choice in movies; actually, she was *looking* more at her perfectly manicured nails than at the screen.

This was exactly the kind of mistake that he and Lavinia frequently made about each other's taste, Max realized. He shuddered, remembering the fake smile and forced cheer with which Lavinia had greeted the simple gold lavaliere he had gotten her for her last birthday.

He hadn't seen it since then either.

"Max, do we have to watch this utter nonsense?" Lavinia asked, raising her nose. "I mean, honestly, this is just so *childish*. Look." She pointed at the screen, at a many-eyed alien creature with gunk coming out of the side of its head.

Max glanced at Lavinia instead. *Childish.* Sometimes he wished Lavinia *would* act a little kid-like. Somewhat subdued since her parents' death a few years ago, Lavinia rarely laughed or acted spontaneously unless she was reacting to a lovely tea or a new china pattern. As usual, she was dressed in impeccable wool slacks and a matching cashmere sweater set. To watch a video on a Thursday night, mind you. Just once he'd like to see her in sweats and a pair of his too-big-for-her trainers, her blond hair in a ponytail. Ha. That would be the day.

Max could picture Elizabeth drooling over Bruce Willis and jumping up and down every time some spaceship exploded. But that was probably because she was American, and Bruce Willis was a major American film star. Then again, one of the things that Max liked so much about Elizabeth was that she probably preferred her journal and the quiet back garden of Pennington House to aliens and explosions.

Elizabeth. His family's kitchen maid. An American in the outskirts of London. A girl with dough under her nails and tomato-sauce stains on her uniform. A girl whose warmth and compassion and kindness radiated from her sweet face.

A girl he couldn't stop thinking about.

It was ironic. At his side sat the girl who history, family, and—if you believed his father—*destiny* had provided for him. Max flicked his eyes at his fiancée. With her swanlike neck and porcelain complexion, Lavinia was inarguably beautiful. She was also, Max knew very well, cultured, intelligent, witty, and—by any measure—a good catch.

But she left him cold.

You've got to face the fact that you've got a monster crush on the scullery maid, mate, Max thought, restraining himself from groaning aloud. As much as he wanted to pretend it wasn't happening, the fact was that his affections—and admiration—for Elizabeth were only growing by the day.

"We're not watching another one," Lavinia said, her expression one of disgust. "I watched one because I know you like this sort of thing. But one's enough."

Max shrugged. He really didn't care. "Um, let's just watch television."

Lavinia rose gracefully and leaned down over the VCR, trying to force it to rewind. "Ugh—I can never remember how to work this thing," she muttered.

As Lavinia cursed the VCR, Max's thoughts did an immediate 180 back to Elizabeth. He knew it wasn't simply a physical thing with her because if that were so, he—and any red-blooded male—would be fantastically satisfied with Lavinia. It was true that Elizabeth was unbelievably fetching—especially when a lock of hair fell out of her ponytail and into her face, as it often did when she was serving at table. . . .

"Max," Lavinia said, clearly not for the first time.

"Yes," Max responded crisply, to make up for the fact that he hadn't answered right away. *This little ruse is working now,* he thought. *But it's not going to work for the next fifty years, now, is it?*

Lavinia gestured at the screen, which was filled with snow. "Fascinated by all the patterns?" she asked sarcastically, tapping her foot with impatience. "What do we want to watch, Max?"

Max flinched at Lavinia's unconscious use of *we.* But since he'd begun dating Lavinia a month before her parents were killed in a car accident, he had developed a ready-made answer for this kind of question. "Whatever you want," he answered, trying to sound hearty and not halfhearted.

Lavinia frowned. "You're on the moon tonight,"

she observed, shaking her head. Then she flopped back on the couch and began channel surfing.

Max's thoughts spun back to Elizabeth. So it *wasn't* only a physical thing. It was something . . . ineffable. Max knew that it had something to do with the spunk—the spark—he admired in Americans. Elizabeth had left her country—and, presumably, all her friends and family—behind, with no plans, lodgings, or people in the place where she was going to see her through.

Max wondered what it would be like to leave his entire superstructure—Lavinia, his thesis, Pennington House, the earl—behind.

"We're watching *Prime Suspect*," Lavinia snapped, settling on the popular police series with relief, clearly having exhausted her patience with the BBC. "Yes, I *know* we've seen this one already."

Max flicked an admiring glance toward the actress Helen Mirren. She was leaning over a table, interrogating a suspect, as usual. Slowly her face merged with Elizabeth's, and it was the kitchen maid hanging over the table, giving some shady character the what-for.

That's what it is, Max suddenly realized. *That's what I like about Elizabeth. Her courage.*

When he and Elizabeth had talked in the garden earlier today, Max had realized that Elizabeth had completely left behind her old life for a new one. It couldn't be easy for her, an intelligent American girl, to be stuck fetching and carrying for a stuffy English family. Yet she handled all her tasks—as far as Max could see—with grace and aplomb. And she clearly hadn't left her goals behind in America either. Every other time he looked, she was out in the garden, writing in her journal.

Max thought of his own thesis with dread. It was all he could do to turn on his computer to look at it every day. He knew that it must not help that each day he worked on his thesis, he was one day closer to taking his father's place in Parliament and marrying Lavinia. And his dream of writing a great novel? Ha! It was stuffed—in the form of several notebooks filled with idiotic scribblings—in some drawer in the back of his bureau.

And that's all it will ever be, probably, Max thought helplessly. *Scribblings.*

"Oh, and Edward and I had the most awful time today," Lavinia said, giggling. She had muted *Prime Suspect* so that the cops and robbers jerked silently around on-screen. "We had to find this citation, and it was in the back of this horrible dusty cabinet. . . ."

Max realized that—again—Lavinia had been talking for some time without his paying attention. She must be talking about work in the auction house. But who was this Edward? It seemed to his ear that Lavinia had mentioned him a couple of times in the past ten minutes or so.

"What's Edward's position again?" Max asked, trying to sound like he had been absorbed in her chatter and not in thoughts of Elizabeth.

Lavinia smacked him lightly on the knee. "I told you," she said. "He's the curator's nephew, but he's very intelligent nonetheless. He's been doing this type of thing for quite a while, actually—"

Max zoned out again—he couldn't help it. Lavinia's job as a curator's assistant was more the social organizing and charity work her mother, the countess, had done before her death. Lavinia wasn't exactly punching a time clock or paying her dues.

When Max had proposed to her, Lavinia had been quiet, subdued, still in shock. Max had been moved by her apparent helplessness—moved enough to think that marriage might be the best solution to both his restlessness and her grief. And his father's pressure to propose had made up Max's mind.

But now Lavinia was acting like a normal twenty-year-old—talkative, interested in her work—even suffering from minor workplace crushes, if Max's view of this "Edward" was correct. And Max was still drifting, rudderless in both his work and his heart—and having a crush on the scullery maid was *not* going to help resolve his difficulties.

"What do you think about orchids, Max?" Lavinia pressed.

Clearly oblivious to Max's interior perturbations, Lavinia had moved onto wedding discussions. Lavinia had become truly obsessed with all the pomp and circumstance of the wedding—it was as if she hoped to fill any gaps in her life. The wedding was to be held at Pennington House in three months, at Christmas, as Lavinia wished, and Lavinia was debating between small sprays of yellow orchids and large, fiery tiger lilies.

Max couldn't care less if it was held in a Tube station during rush hour. "Tiger lilies are nice," Max offered, although he had no idea what they were.

"Yes," Lavinia murmured. "But orchids are so exquisite. . . ."

Max suddenly caught a vision of his and Lavinia's future: He safely ensconced in the library of Pennington House, going over old Greek and Latin books while he puffed soberly on a cigar; she safely tucked away in some wing, going over fabric swatches for one of her many sweeping renovations. A tidy couple, in a tidy castle, locked up for the rest of their lives.

Why don't we serve them some Indian take-away, recite our vows off index cards, and call it a day? Max had to restrain himself from shouting.

Lavinia had wandered off to her bedroom to

find one of the hundreds of catalogs and magazines she had arrayed for this purpose. She returned with a flower magazine and began to pore over it, her brow furrowed in concentration. On the cover a plastic-looking bride gazed serenely up at her faceless husband.

Was that all this crush on Elizabeth was? A desperate last-ditch effort to avoid being crushed into what seemed to Max more like an advertisement for marriage than the real thing?

No, Max mused. Even though he wished it were only a passing fancy, he was truly taken with this girl. She was so spirited, so independent, so . . . everything Lavinia was not.

On the screen a man backed slowly away from a bunch of toughs armed with rifles. He raised his hands in panic. "Nooo!" he screamed as the criminals let loose and fired.

Max knew exactly how the man felt. In fact, at that moment he would have happily traded places with him.

Elizabeth Wakefield hurled the last bucket of steaming water over the stone floor of the kitchen, then straightened up and groaned. Argh. These old kitchens were totally astonishing: Elizabeth was sure she would never get over the difference between the sleek, metallic, Windex-ready kitchen where she had grown up and this—this *relic* from Victorian England.

Part of Elizabeth's last duty in the evening was to rinse and scrub down everything: the ancient huge table in the middle on which Cook and Mary performed all of their duties, the enormous black stove, the original stone floor that Elizabeth was sure hadn't changed a whit since the kitchen was originally built. In fact, Elizabeth was sure that *very* little had changed since the kitchen was originally built, except for the added deep freeze, gas grill, and intercom—which mainly existed, as far as Elizabeth could tell, for Sarah, Pennington House's sixteen-year-old mistress, to call down every fifteen minutes for more fat-free scones.

Elizabeth took the hard-backed wooden brush from her bucket of tools and got down on her hands and knees to give the floor one last scrub down. In her early days on the job, she had been sure that the onerous tasks were going to immediately overwhelm her, not to mention some of the "quainter" cleaning implements. Although Mary's arsenal was stocked with three nine-hundred-dollar Miele vacuum cleaners, Elizabeth was often stuck using tools that were made, she was sure, for ladies wearing stays and lace hats. Sometimes she was surprised that she didn't have to sweep out each room with a brush made of thistle while ladies in waiting were serenaded by some traveling minstrel.

But—blisters aside—Elizabeth had actually come to find the work calming. There was nothing to make you forget a cheating sister and boyfriend like twenty grates to sweep out before nine o'clock in the morning.

Ugh. Sam and Jessica. Sam. And Jessica. Elizabeth was amazed how painful the names still were to her. Even if she had to scrub down twenty more floors every day, she would have done so happily if the task could only remove the terrible, deep kick of sorrow she still felt at the thought of her sister and Sam kissing in the awful hotel room.

Elizabeth shoved the last bit of rubbish into the grate and stood slowly, fighting tears. She looked down at her hands. They were red, rough, and swollen, dotted with bleeding calluses—a far cry from the mildly ink-stained forefinger she used to get in school from writing so often. Here she wrote, but it was in between dust mopping the living room and hauling away Cook's stacks of vegetable choppings. Elizabeth rubbed her hand slowly down her chinos, wincing slightly. If only her insides didn't feel the same way.

It was strange—that horrifying image of Jessica kissing Sam deeply on the lips cropped up at the strangest times: late at night, while she was turning down her bed; in the morning, over the ubiquitous toast and tea; in the middle of the afternoon, when Elizabeth was depositing the last of a filthy stack of dishes from lunch into the chasmlike sink.

But that's no reason to dwell on it, Elizabeth thought, replacing her bucket back in the closet and rinsing her hands briefly under the well-scrubbed faucet. She shook her head and breathed in deeply the scent of the now completely dry stone floor, trying to focus. *C'mon. You're thousands of miles away, in a country where people think Marmite is* food, Elizabeth berated herself. *Sam and Jessica couldn't be farther away.*

As far as Elizabeth's thoughts were concerned, however, they might have been in the next room. Her thoughts proceeded completely without her approval. She began to think of all the other people she had lost on her trip to England—*and Sam and Jess were quite enough, thank you very much,* Elizabeth thought. Nina Harper, for instance. Leaning against the sink, Elizabeth winced at the thought of her best friend from Sweet Valley University, who she had left back in the United States without so much as a parting word.

What I would give for a late night Chee-tos-and-study session with Nina, Elizabeth thought, tears crowding her eyes. She swiped them away angrily.

You've got to put all that behind you now,

Elizabeth. Just like you've put your real name be-hind you.

Elizabeth thought back to the evening she'd first arrived at Pennington House; she'd been nervous about giving her real name, just in case someone from her past should try to track her down. And so she'd told the people at Pennington House that her name was Elizabeth *Bennet*.

Elizabeth Bennet, the heroine of *Pride and Prejudice,* one of Elizabeth's favorite novels.

Elizabeth sniffed and knelt down, picking up nonexistent bits of dust from the floor and stove. God, that Jess-and-Sam thing sure had come out of left field, hadn't it? *I mean, everyone knew that Jess was a flirt—and arguably more competitive than the U.S. women's soccer team. Sam could also be inconsiderate. But . . . c'mon.* Those traits had heretofore expressed themselves in Jessica being sure to be the first person to wear on Monday whatever had hit the stores on Saturday and Sam's frequently leaving empty milk cartons in the fridge.

It didn't exactly add up to *Dangerous Liaisons.* Still, it had happened, so there had to be a reason. Elizabeth hadn't done anything to encourage them to fool around, had she?

Nothing more than be born with a twin sister who was—evidently—a perfectly acceptable stand-in for me in an intimate relationship, Elizabeth

14

thought bitterly. It was strange: One part of her wished she *had* done something blatant to encourage the affair—*Like what? Say what a great kisser Jess was to Sam?* Elizabeth thought with annoyance—because then, at least, she would have an explanation for Jessica and Sam's behavior. As it was, she had let her misery propel her to England and churn in her stomach for over a month, and she was no closer to an answer.

I wonder if Mom and Dad have figured out what happened by now, Elizabeth wondered. The last time she had seen them, they were accosting her in the airport, screaming at her furiously for leaving her sister stranded in a motel in the middle of nowhere. Elizabeth had been so traumatized that she'd been unable to respond—she'd simply slung her backpack over her shoulder and headed onto the plane, not even stopping to look back.

Now, whenever she thought of her parents, a pain cut across her chest as sharply as a knife.

Well, I'm sure Jessica *didn't clue them in to the actual savory details,* Elizabeth thought. *Still, they're pretty swift. They know it's not really like me to leave Jess up the creek without a paddle—even though I've definitely wanted to a thousand times.*

Strangely, the thought of Jessica deserted and penniless in the middle of nowhere—even momentarily—never gave Elizabeth any satisfaction.

It was as if that person Elizabeth had seen with Sam wasn't Jessica at all. She was a total stranger to Elizabeth, and it didn't matter if she was left alone to foot the motel bill—or left alone to broil in the middle of the Mojave Desert.

Elizabeth realized she was folding and refolding a stack of tea towels with brutal efficiency. Unable to stop a sob from coming forward, she pressed one of the crisp white rectangles briefly to her face and let her tears flow. After one or two good sobs she blew her nose into the stiff linen, then walked over to drop it into the laundry bin under the cabinet with as much dignity as she could muster.

Suddenly Mary, head housekeeper and Elizabeth's boss, appeared at the door. Elizabeth's hands flew to her cheeks for a second—would Mary be able to tell that she had been weeping on the clock? She caught a semiglimpse of herself in the side of one of the steely pots hanging over the sink. Probably not, Elizabeth realized. After she finished a normal day of work, she was usually so red and wet and scraggly, she could have cried through ten screenings of *Titanic* and it would be impossible for anyone to notice the difference.

"Very satisfactory," Mary observed, giving Elizabeth a small nod. She turned and left. Elizabeth couldn't help but feel a small flush of pride. Gosh, traveling thousands of miles from home sure did wonders for the fluidity of one's identity, didn't it? *I mean*, Elizabeth thought, *at home I was just another struggling student with a boyfriend and dreams of being a writer. Now I'm a scullery maid!*

Elizabeth knew that she joked about the maid thing not from anxiety—she knew she wouldn't stay a maid forever—but to keep her mind off how desperately changed her circumstances had become in just one short month.

Elizabeth rationalized her circumstances thus: In a sense, it was *good* that the school hadn't ever received a confirmation letter from Elizabeth to keep her place in the writing program. (Picturing herself happily ensconced in a writing nook in a Tudor-style dorm, happily attending rugby matches, Elizabeth's rationalizing always got a little shaky.) There, everyone would have been able to locate her—she would have been hounded by the world she was trying to leave behind. Here, there wasn't a soul from her old life who knew where she was or what she was doing. The only problem was, Elizabeth sometimes felt like she had dropped off the edge of the world.

Elizabeth put a few sticks into the coal basket to prepare the kitchen's fire for tomorrow (the fire was actually used for everything from toasting to baking, to Elizabeth's eternal amusement). Calls from Sam and Jessica were the last thing Elizabeth wanted right now. There was absolutely no excuse—could *not* be an excuse—for what they had done.

Elizabeth wiped her hands on her shirt and headed up the back stairway, toward the servants' quarters.

With problems like these at home, Elizabeth thought ruefully, feeling every joint in her body crack in protest as she ascended the four flights, *it's no wonder I'm really grateful for hard labor.*

Sarah Pennington was bored. Bored, bored, bored, and bored. While it was true that practically living under house arrest had given her plenty of time to catalog Prince William's love interests—*Whatever! I'm the one Wills fancies,* Sarah had concluded after a few flips through *Jump* magazine—it certainly wasn't a snog session in a deserted classroom with Nick. Which was, frankly, all she had been able to think about for the past couple of days.

Sex! Nick actually expected them to have sex! Sarah's stomach gave a little flip each time she even *thought* the word. *It seems mad to think of me and sex in the same sentence,* Sarah thought, looking down at her perfectly flat stomach as if it held monsters that would shortly emerge to eat her alive. *For God's sake, I'm only sixteen!*

Still, it's not an opportunity I should really pass

up, should I? Sarah thought, almost shivering with delight. *Nick's so hot, and he's such a good kisser.*

Sarah leaned back against a heap of pillows, almost losing herself in a reverie about her and Nick's last secret tryst. Nick had traced her profile with his finger, very gently, causing Sarah's arms to break out in goose pimples while she practically swooned in delight.

But what if Father finds out? the practical side of Sarah suddenly interjected. Sarah sat straight up in bed. Father . . . *knowing* that she was *having sex?* She looked at the full-length poster of the prince on the far wall. The thought of the earl *knowing* about her and Nick—and the fury that would surely erupt from him, like twenty Mount Saint Helens—was enough to make Sarah wish that she was one of the girls slated to marry the prince. Even if he was growing to look a little bit like a stork.

Dad's not going to find out, Sarah tried to reassure herself. She smoothed down her lace-eyelet coverlet. *How could he?*

Well, he could send someone to follow you around, Sarah's practical side countered again.

Sarah had to practically put her hands over her mouth to keep from speaking aloud. *Bosh! He's not that worried,* she thought confidently.

Still, she would have to be very, very careful.

Sarah looked at the phone with longing. If only Victoria were home! They could have a heart-to-heart about V-day (as Sarah had taken to calling the day she very well might lose her virginity) and go over the plans to get Sarah safely out of Pennington House and into Nick's place.

But unfortunately, Victoria was stuck at some boring and stuffy dinner with her parents, who were entertaining the visiting heads of Tweezledump and Lumperdink or whatever the strange foreign countries were that Victoria had recited, giggling, over the phone. Victoria's father was a diplomat, and Victoria was always stuck having to be friendly to foreigners in strange hats while her father and mother chatted gamely with them across the table.

Who else could she call? Not Nick—they didn't have that kind of relationship. (Anyway, she couldn't very well call up Nick to talk about *Nick*, could she?) Max was stuck with the ice queen, Lavinia, for the night—probably having some dumb conversation about whether or not to force-feed or straitjacket the guests with flowers while the couple consumed sherry and crackers, like they were both already a thousand years old. The maids at Pennington House? Sarah let out a bark of laughter. Maybe she could call them all on the intercom and tell them she'd pay them each five quid if they could help her escape the house on Saturday to lose her virginity.

The ludicrousness of her situation buoyed Sarah's spirits. There was no sense grumping

20

around, was there? She still had TV, didn't she? She'd put something on and just try to forget about Nick until tomorrow.

Like that will happen, Sarah could picture Victoria saying scornfully, twirling one of her curly locks around her finger.

Sarah began to go through all her videos. Unfortunately, she'd really already watched all of them, especially some of the videotapes of the Spice Girls in concert. She'd nearly worn those out on the spools of the VCR last summer, playing them over and over again to learn dance moves that by now were defunct. She threw them all on the floor in disgust—the Spice Girls were only for twelve-year-olds, really.

Sarah came across one video still in a plastic wrapper, lifted it out, and frowned. On the front was a picture of a redheaded girl in an extremely puffy wedding gown, smiling widely. *Muriel's Wedding* was scrawled across the front in fancy script.

Suddenly Sarah remembered where she'd gotten the tape. Lavinia, the walking ice sculpture, had given the tape to her for her birthday last year. Sarah had assumed it was some stupid wedding video and tossed it aside in annoyance, thinking that it was just like Lavinia to make everything about weddings. Since, Sarah had realized it was a regular movie—and evidently a funny one. She just hadn't had time to watch it.

Well, she certainly had time now, didn't she? Flicking out the main lamps, Sarah crumpled the plastic wrapper into the garbage can and fed the VCR the unused tape.

For the next two hours Sarah sat speechless, mesmerized. The movie made her want to move to Australia straightaway. *I mean, here's a girl—and kind of a fat girl, at that,* Sarah thought, immediately feeling better about the two scones she'd eaten for breakfast—*doing whatever she wants despite what her parents said.* She was living out on her own, taking the consequences for her actions, even if they were sometimes totally unexpected.

Having, Sarah thought swiftly, *a life.*

As the movie wound to a close, Sarah was so moved that she practically jumped up and clapped. She felt like the movie was exactly the boost she had needed for her situation with Nick—a sign, Sarah decided, that it was time to start making her own decisions.

I mean, I'm almost an adult now, right? Sarah thought, listening to the machine rewinding the tape speed up to a crescendo, then slow and whir to a stop. *In fact, I have to start making decisions myself if I'm ever going to have the fabulous life I know I was born for.*

And I've got the perfect one to start with. But first, I've got to make sure Daddy is busy worrying about other things than well-behaved, virginal me. . . .

Chapter Two

The next morning Elizabeth pulled six strips of bacon off a rasher and arranged them artfully on a plate, leaning past Cook to add a sprig of parsley.

"Miss Sarah's going to eat the entire pig before long if she keeps this up," Cook observed sagely, rolling out chicken cutlets in flour before she smeared them with an indefinable substance.

Elizabeth tried to be diplomatic. "Well, she's a growing girl."

Cook, who was quite a formidable woman herself, rolled a cutlet energetically and deposited it in the broiling pan. "She'll grow, all right," Elizabeth heard as she exited through the swinging doors. She didn't need to wait for Cook's eternal punch line: "In all the wrong directions!"

It *was* strange, Elizabeth thought as she headed toward the dining room, almost unconsciously assuming the erect, yet submissive posture that Mary, Vanessa, and all the other servants seemed to hold constantly without even thinking about it. *Sarah's either got some dog upstairs that she's saving scraps for,* Elizabeth reasoned, *or she's working on some scheme.*

For the past couple of days Sarah had been calling Elizabeth into the dining room almost every other minute, usually for something that was later found to be on the table, like yesterday's raspberry jam or today's rasher of bacon—which Elizabeth was sure she would find artfully concealed under a napkin as soon as she cleared the table.

What was Sarah up to, then? Whatever it was, it had something to do with Max—who gave Elizabeth enough flutters every time she caught his crooked half grin aimed at her anyway. Also, every time she came in, Elizabeth mused, Sarah made sure to engage her in conversation, often beginning them out of the blue, with queries like: "What kind of sports did you play growing up, Elizabeth?" or, "Do all American boys really say 'dude' and wear plaid shirts and baseball caps all the time, like in the movies?"

Elizabeth would endeavor to answer as briefly as possible, ever heedful of the earl, who, after a suitable period of time, would rattle his paper, clear his throat loudly, and interrupt whatever follow-up question Sarah had invented with a terse: "That will be all."

But in the interim, Sarah did whatever she could to draw Max into the conversation with her and Elizabeth. If Elizabeth said she had grown up playing soccer on the fields of California, Sarah would nudge Max and say, "See? I told you Americans love football." If Elizabeth confirmed that American boys did, indeed, primarily dress in plaid shirts and baseball caps, Sarah would cock her head in Max's direction and say, "Don't you like English boys better?"

Perhaps Sarah was just sporting with her; "taking the piss," as Vanessa, the other scullery maid, would say. It was true that some particular comments had, indeed, made her blush—she had been deeply grateful for the earl's "That will be all." It had been all she could do to keep from blurting out, "Yes, I do—particularly that English boy!"

Elizabeth entered the sunny dining room, prepared for the immediate buzz of amusement that followed her appearance. Even the earl, Elizabeth was sure, was starting to find these little visitations slightly funny, even if his *thank-yous* and *that will be alls* went completely ignored by Sarah.

"Here you are," Elizabeth said as soberly as possible, taking the napkin off the plate of bacon, placing it in front of Sarah, and heading for the door as quickly as possible—managing to avoid the eyes of anyone who might be trying to catch her own. Unfortunately, the dining room was large, and in the time it took her to traverse it, Sarah stopped her with a ringing question.

"Elizabeth?" Sarah asked, letting her name hang in the air. Elizabeth turned and looked at her as politely as she could manage. She was pretty sure that Sarah hadn't even formulated the question she was going to ask yet—the brat! She tried to avoid looking at Max—Elizabeth was certain he looked as adorable as he always did this morning, but she needed to maintain her composure now, not dissolve into a blush of high-school-girl giggles.

Vanessa came into the room, bearing the teapot, and began to move around the table, hiding a smile as she refreshed everyone's beverages. Vanessa had warned Elizabeth repeatedly about allowing familiarities with the family when Elizabeth had first joined the staff and now took great pleasure in her daily tortures. "That will be all," Vanessa had taken to cracking as Alice went to switch out the lights so all three maids could go to bed, to the great amusement of Alice and to the great embarrassment of Elizabeth.

"What would you say is the primary difference between American and English lawn care?" Sarah asked.

Elizabeth had to hold in her sides to keep from cracking up. Sarah had been asking some—as they said over here—*queer* questions lately, but nothing quite this bizarre. Max tossed down his section of the paper and let out a hearty bark of a laugh, folding his arms up in an I've-got-to-see-what-she-does-with-this-one posture.

Elizabeth put on a poker face, deciding to answer the question as straightforwardly as possible. In English films that was what butlers did, wasn't it? Attempted to accede to any employer request, however bizarre? Today Elizabeth would behave like an English butler.

"Well," Elizabeth began, "I'd say that Americans are more concerned with the green of the grass and the English with the red of the rose."

Max looked impressed. The earl, Elizabeth saw, had even pricked up his ears. Was that a hint of amusement crinkling the corners of his mouth? Sarah sat, momentarily rendered speechless by Elizabeth's confident return of her conversational parry. She took a piece of bacon and chewed it thoughtfully.

"That will be all," Vanessa mouthed widely as she passed Elizabeth, immediately masking her features again as she passed within view of the family. Elizabeth had to fight the impulse to goose Vanessa for threatening to break down her hard-won, butlerlike dignity.

"Well," Sarah asked, her voice taking on a curious lilt, "I only mentioned it because you spend so much time in the garden. I wanted to know if you like English ones or American ones better."

Elizabeth softened immediately. Could it be that the girl was looking for an older-sister figure? The constant forays into conversation; the not-so-subtle pleas for Elizabeth to like Max too—it would all fit. And Elizabeth knew that Sarah's mother had died when she was younger—perhaps this incessant querying was just a cry for female companionship.

"Well," Elizabeth said warmly, "the lawns in America are better for Frisbee, but the gardens here are wonderful for writing."

Sarah gave Elizabeth a dimpled, innocent grin. "Do you think you could beat Max in Frisbee?" she said impishly.

Action suddenly broke out on all sides. Max picked up his paper again and rustled it ominously. Mary came in through the side door and looked at Elizabeth darkly, her brow cut with disapproval—*Attempting to socialize with the family again?* it seemed to say. The earl looked up at Elizabeth, his eyes like the sockets of the cold, dead fish that Cook gutted and dressed almost every day after they were delivered fresh from market. Elizabeth almost wanted to raise her hands and conduct a chorus of everyone reciting the earl's familiar dismissal: "That will be all."

As Elizabeth gave a slight bow and moved toward the door, she heard the earl clear his throat. "Max, my boy," he began, and Elizabeth could hear that he had put down the paper. He must be looking directly at Max. "What time will the duchess and her aunt and uncle be here tomorrow?" he asked.

Elizabeth felt the familiar pang of disappointment that came with every mention of the duchess. *God, Elizabeth, get over it, will you?* she berated herself. *He's royalty, and you're just a servant. All this is is a stupid crush, and you shouldn't take it more seriously than that crush on that Backstreet Boy you had in the ninth grade.*

Smiling at the memory of the full-length picture of the Backstreet Boys that had once adorned her closet door, Elizabeth couldn't help but strain to hear Max's reply. As the door closed, swinging behind her, Elizabeth caught his muffled response: "Six, Dad," Max said, clearly still chewing. "I told you already."

See? Get with the program, Elizabeth, she told herself. *Those conversations in the garden don't mean anything—he's just being friendly. He's already got a fiancée—a real lady in waiting too—a duchess!*

Elizabeth made her way back to the kitchen as swiftly as she could, wondering what the fiancée looked like. A true English rose, like Sarah? Or perhaps she would be haggard and partly toothless, exactly like the evil stepsisters in *Cinderella*.

Whatever she looks like, Elizabeth thought, *I don't relish the thought of having to lean over her and spoon peas onto her plate.*

Elizabeth shuddered. She had certainly come a long way from the fourteen-year-old who had stood up on her tippy toes to kiss pop stars' grinning visages every night—but not exactly in the direction she would have thought.

Elizabeth entered the warm, bustling kitchen and tried to look as expressionless as possible when Alice and Vanessa both raised their eyebrows. "Elizabeth," Mary said in a steely voice. "I'd like you to wash the blinds after you're finished with your duties in the kitchen today."

Cinderella, indeed. Elizabeth could feel the bruises already.

"Remember," Mary continued. "When you are serving the family, try to be prompt and efficient. Our job is not to stand idly by and chatter."

Mary could be a little more sympathetic, Elizabeth thought with irritation. What was she supposed to do—pretend she was deaf when Sarah shouted across the room?

On the other hand, Elizabeth thought, it *was* true that her American gregariousness seemed to get her into trouble. Vanessa looked like she might bite the head of anyone who spoke to her and answered all questions with a nearly inaudible "Yes, miss," or "No, sir." The family tiptoed around her accordingly.

Elizabeth suspected that Vanessa acted so blank to prevent any undue involvement with the family breaking down her wall of self-protection. *But why does she need to be so secret?* Elizabeth thought, unable to drop her old journalist habits, even when she was up to her elbows in dirty dishes and tea towels. *What does she have to hide?*

Elizabeth rolled up her sleeves and tried to concentrate on the task at hand: sorting the silver before the breakfast dishes came in. *I might do well to put up some castle walls myself,* Elizabeth thought, lining the tines of each fork up neatly with the one below. *Because even though I feel like Cinderella sometimes, I'm pretty sure that in this version of the story the scullery maid doesn't end up with the prince.*

Sarah clutched her stomach and lay on her bed, groaning. Argh! She was going to have to find some other way to push Max and Elizabeth together—this constant arrival of food was going to have her looking like the Queen Mother any minute. (And unlike her, Sarah thought, she didn't even get to take the occasional celebratory slug of gin.)

Her evil plan was working, though—she could see that Max was starting to look forward to these question-and-answer sessions with Elizabeth at the breakfast table. And Elizabeth obviously loved any opportunity to be in close proximity to Max— Sarah didn't care how serious an expression she contorted her face into whenever Sarah cornered her.

Sarah stood up and started jumping up and down rapidly, counting off one calorie per five jumps. Once Elizabeth and Max were into some hot and heavy love affair, Daddy would be so busy watching Max and yelling at him and worrying about whether the wedding of the new century would ever take place that he'd barely have time to notice that Sarah was sneaking out every night to meet hot Nick!

Before she even started to breathe heavily, however, Sarah got bored and flopped back down on the bed. Across the room her image looked back at her dolefully from within the confines of a gold-leaf frame from God knew where. This mirror made her look greenish. Sarah stood and pinched her waist carefully. She looked at herself sideways, sucking in her stomach. She wasn't gaining weight already from all those Elizabeth snacks, was she?

Nonsense, Sarah decided. That slight hint of new flesh was just the heinous, awful, tacky school uniforms they were forced to wear at her exclusive girls' school.

Sarah glanced at the clock. She had just enough time to ring Victoria and have a high-speed heart-to-heart about how to handle Nick before school. Sarah hit the speed dial that connected her directly to Victoria's private line and flipped over on the bed, raising her legs against the wall so that she could examine her knees.

Uch. Pretty knobby, she concluded as she waited for Victoria to pick up.

After an incredibly long series of rings, in Sarah's opinion, she finally heard Victoria's voice on the other end of the line. "Hello?" Victoria said breathlessly.

Sarah didn't restrain herself. "Vic, you idiot, where've you been?" she blasted. "I've been ringing you for over an hour."

Victoria swallowed and appeared to drop the phone. When she picked it up again, she sounded like her voice was coming from very far away. "Hi," Victoria said, clearly still chewing something. "We were at breakfast," she added.

Sarah had no time for preliminaries. "Well, plant your head back on your shoulders because

33

we've got to think of a plan," she hissed, trying to keep her voice down in case Mary or her father was lurking near her door.

Victoria swallowed again. "A plan?" she said. "For what?"

Sarah wanted to travel through the phone wires and bash Victoria on the head with her receiver. "Don't be so thick, all right?" she complained. "I need your help with Nick."

Victoria appeared to rally. "Oh, yes!" she practically screamed. "Tomorrow's the big day!"

Sarah couldn't help but cut her eyes toward the door before answering. "We think," she said, trying to sound noncommittal, as if she lost her virginity on a weekly basis. "But I don't know how I'm going to get out of here, Vic!" she said, switching tacks quickly.

Victoria was silent a moment. "Why not just say you're going to come study with me?" she said finally. "Then arrange to meet Nick here, and you'll go off, and if your dad calls or sends anyone round, I'll say you've gone out to get us some frozen yogurt."

Sarah was silent, allowing all the perambulations of the plan to resolve in her brain before she gave her assent. "You know what, Vic?" she asked.

"What?" Victoria asked dutifully.

Sarah was practically beside herself with joy. "I

think that's just stupid enough to work!"

Victoria popped the last of something in her mouth—this time it sounded like an apple. "Brilliant," she said as she chewed.

The girls said their good-byes, and Sarah propped her legs back up. *These are the legs that Nick is going to see tomorrow,* Sarah thought, barely able to contain both the fear and the deliciousness of the thought.

The back of her neck began to ache. Sarah flipped back over on the bed, knocking over an enormous pile of books and papers. "Oh, blast," she muttered, leaning over. *I've probably got to start using a better filing system than this one anyhow,* she thought, looking at the heap of schoolbooks, old papers, letters, magazines, and—was that glitter glue?—that now littered half the floor.

"Blast," Sarah muttered again, kicking at a sheaf of school papers. They scattered to cover even more of the carpet. From the looks of her handwriting, they had been written about two years ago.

Her kick had also uncovered a plain leather binder. Sarah gasped, remembering. A few months after her mother died, Sarah had been poking around in her father's drawers—being nosy as usual. She hadn't expected to come across a treasure trove of photographs of her old mum, most of them with her and Max when they were infants.

Sarah remembered going through the photographs that day and crying ceaselessly. She had taken them back to her room with her and eventually placed them in an album. That year after her mother's death she had looked at the pictures nearly every day, tracing over the thin plastic covering to the face of her mother forever locked, smiling, beneath.

But Sarah hadn't looked at the album, or thought of it, in years. The earl had never noticed that the pictures were missing—or if he had, he had never mentioned anything about it to Sarah.

Sarah sat down, her chest suddenly feeling like some heavy object—a paperweight or a dictionary, perhaps—had been placed on it. She sighed deeply and turned the first page.

Sarah gave a harsh intake of breath at the image. Her mother was holding baby Sarah up in her arms, smiling widely. It was clearly a posed picture—her mother was dressed richly, with dark lipstick and pearls, and baby Sarah was in some kind of lacy slip, with a small beaded cap crowning her nearly bald head. "There's Mum," Sarah whispered, as if in amazement that her mother's features had remained the same all of these years. "How are you?" she asked the image, which was yellowing under the crinkled plastic that was supposed to protect it.

Sarah turned the page, then the next. Each time she saw a shot, she couldn't believe she had forgotten it this whole time: her mother leaning over her in the bath, offering Sarah a little plastic ducky; both mother and daughter dressed in riding togs, Sarah's mother holding a crop in one hand, the other smoothing Sarah's hair; a clearly impromptu photo taken at her mother's old dressing table, Sarah's thumb in her mouth while Max looked to be doing something unwise with the tray of lipsticks.

Sarah closed the book. "I wish you were here," she murmured, hardly knowing what she had said. She clasped the album to her chest.

Mother, will you help me figure out what to do about Nick?

Vanessa Shaw headed away from Sarah's wing, where, from a quick glance outside at the black Bentley still parked in the gravel driveway, she knew that Sarah was still ensconced.

That brat's going to be late again, Vanessa thought, annoyed that she wasn't going to be able to rifle through Sarah's room straightaway, when she knew everyone else was busy. Vanessa's scourings of the house for evidence of the earl's affair with her mother had become so routine that she automatically filed everyone's hourly schedule throughout the day away in her brain for future sleuthing use.

That goody-goody new maid, Elizabeth Bennet, Vanessa ticked off, was still scrubbing the kitchen floor—and after that she would be busy with Mary's punishment: the endless blinds. The earl was safely ensconced in his library, from where he never emerged before eleven, when he often set off for Parliament. Max had set off with his fiancée, Lavinia, for Harrods—and from what Vanessa had seen of her so far, she was sure that the icy blonde would keep Max busy for hours haggling over duvet covers and crystal bookends.

And Mary's busy deciding the menu (or, as Alice insisted on referring to it, the Big M) *for the wedding,* Vanessa thought with satisfaction. *Just deciding whether those lovely rich geezers should eat leeks and potatoes while they gaze at the lovely couple is sure to take her an hour.*

Mentally gagging at the vision of the house choked with the wealthy, self-satisfied friends of the earl, Vanessa momentarily conjured up an image of the earl himself dressed and trussed like a duck. Heave-ho, she imagined Cook saying, while the two of them plunged him into the red-hot oven.

Now, that's a wedding I'd attend, Vanessa

thought, smiling despite herself. She decided to head to the dusty back wing, which Mary used to store much of the old furniture that had gone out of rotation since the earl's wife's death. *It's mostly junk back there,* Vanessa thought, *but that makes it a good candidate for a hiding place for the earl.*

Looking as busy and occupied as she could manage, Vanessa made her way briskly through the halls, her keys shaking with a little emphatic jingle on each step. She reached the door of the wing and swung open the door to the empty hall, coughing a little at the dust. Although they cleaned these halls routinely, the emptiness still seemed to breed more filth than the rest of the house. *Just like the earl's soul,* Vanessa thought, looking for the drawing-room key.

After unlocking the door of the dusty drawing room, Vanessa covered her face with a handkerchief and walked swiftly over to the windows to pull them open. In case anyone *did* happen upon her, she planned to say that she had simply recalled that these rooms hadn't been aired out in a good three months, and she had thought it high time to make sure none of the furniture was getting wood rot or infested by moths.

Ha! Vanessa thought. *As if anything in this house would have half a second to rot, with its fleet of servants constantly scrubbing everything to within half an inch of its life.*

For the next half hour, although she went over each available surface with an eagle eye, Vanessa found nothing except for several large dust balls and an old ballpoint pen from London's Hyatt Regency—a possible trysting place for her mother and the earl, yes—but hardly damning in and of itself. As she knelt down in front of a large secretary, she caught a glimpse of herself in the cracked mirror border. *Why, I look like I've been rolling in a pile of leaves!* Vanessa thought in surprise, noting her now bedraggled hair, red-rimmed eyes, and look of almost manic intent. She tried quickly to smooth back her hair, then gave up. *Who cares what I look like anyway,* she thought, angry that she had wasted a moment's thought on such frippery. *Look what looks did to my mother.*

Vanessa yanked open the first drawer of the secretary and peered inside. She had another thought. *I wonder if Mum ever saw herself in that mirror?* she wondered. *Perhaps she's the one who broke it.*

Vanessa tried to envision her mother not as she had ever known her, but as the earl must have: young, unburdened, standing with him in whatever room the secretary had originally resided in. She saw the earl smiling, taking her mother's hand, leading her to a seat. She saw her mother's face fall, crumple. She saw her mother pick up a heavy crystal egg and throw it across the room.

Vanessa felt sick to her stomach. *It's not likely Mum broke it,* Vanessa thought, yanking open the last drawer. *It's she who was broken, not the other way round.*

Vanessa stared. A brown, curling piece of paper lay at the bottom of the drawer, half wedged into a seam.

Dear God, let it be the proof I need, Vanessa thought fervently, reaching for the scrap. Her hands trembled as she felt it with the tips of her fingers.

Regency House, the tag read. *£73,000.*

"A stupid receipt!" Vanessa said aloud. She half laughed aloud, letting the piece of paper fall to the floor. *Just an idiotic, silly slip from some store that probably doesn't even exist anymore.*

Vanessa looked around the large, sunny room, which suddenly looked like a graveyard for furniture, all the massive shapes swathed in dull gray canvas in the shadows. She laughed again. What was she doing here? How could she ever find the simple proof she needed in this enormous—almost endless—house? She might as well march into the earl's library and ask if he was her father point-blank. This was a fool's errand.

Still, that's a pretty hefty tag, isn't it? Vanessa

thought, her thoughts refusing to be quelled by the enormity of the task before her. She reached down and held the small slip of paper as if it were a check for that amount, not a receipt. *That's more money than my mother ever saw in her entire life,* Vanessa added to herself, the paper turning to dust in her hands.

"Um, I'm sorry to interrupt," Elizabeth said from the doorway.

Vanessa spun around, nearly choking with fright. She had to remind herself that she wasn't doing anything out of the ordinary—*just kneeling on the floor to pick up a piece of rubbish,* Vanessa thought, rising to her feet and fixing Elizabeth with as uninterested a gaze as she could muster. *Just cleaning out an old wing.*

"What is it?" Vanessa asked, trying to sound haughty and imperious, as if Elizabeth had interrupted her in the middle of a delicate surgical procedure.

Elizabeth responded appropriately, a flush of shame rising to her cheeks as she practically stammered her apology. "I didn't mean to trouble you," Elizabeth said, clutching what looked to Vanessa like a pail of dirty mop water. *She must have started on the blinds already,* Vanessa thought. *Except there are no blinds at all here!*

"I just seem to have misplaced the living room," Elizabeth finished.

All anxieties vanished. The new maid was *lost;* that was all, Vanessa realized. She wasn't here to spy for Mary. In fact, she was frightened, Vanessa decided, looking at Elizabeth's tense, furrowed brow, that *Vanessa* would report *her* to Mary.

I better act friendly, thought Vanessa. *She may be a bit timid, but I need as many allies as I can find if I'm going to be running about through the entire house like a bloodhound.*

"Don't worry," Vanessa said smoothly, putting her arm through Elizabeth's and reaching for the mop bucket. "I'll show you myself."

Elizabeth couldn't contain her joy. "Oh, thanks so much!" she burbled, looking as thrilled as if Vanessa had just presented her with a set of diamond earrings. *What a sap*, Vanessa thought, trying to keep a smile on her face.

"Oh, it's all right," Vanessa continued. "When I first came here, I misplaced the kitchen for an entire week." She laughed warmly—she hoped—with Elizabeth. "And Mary was none too pleased, let me tell you . . ."

Chapter Three

Lavinia lifted the edge of the beige duvet—"eggshell, actually," the personal shopper, Hamish, had corrected Max moments before—and held it up for Max's inspection, giving it a little shake to take out the wrinkles. "Well, what do you think?" she asked finally, a worried frown creasing the space between her eyebrows.

Holding the heavy fabric aloft, Lavinia looked vaguely Greek. "I think you would make a wonderful Athena," Max offered, trying for a little levity.

Lavinia scowled and flung the duvet on top of the heaping pile of linens, then strode off toward the china section, followed by a fluttering Hamish, the man Harrods had assigned to them for the morning, to Max's consternation.

Max sighed. So far, the last five minutes had

been the high point of the morning, actually. The minute they had arrived—greeted by Hamish, dressed in a sleek gray suit and two-toned shoes, with an expensive sheen on his oddly egg-shaped head—Lavinia's cheeks had borne the red pinpoint that indicated she was on the edge of losing her temper.

Max took responsibility for some of it. He had picked her up twenty minutes late that morning and, come to think of it, canceled this Harrods trip twice already—but otherwise he had tried to be amiable. As they had walked through the gleaming, bustling halls, he had made what he deemed appropriate murmurs of approval whenever Lavinia held up a soup tureen or laid out an arrangement of silver patterns. So he had sneaked off once briefly for a biscotti when Hamish and Lavinia were arguing over swags. (*What in the world,* Max had thought, creeping away, *are swags, and why do I have to have them in my house?*) And when he'd returned from his biscotti mission, he had brought Lavinia back a double espresso in a large cup, just the way she liked it, hadn't he?

But Max knew the hammer was falling as Lavinia silently accepted his offering. She was, Max realized, only barely containing the urge to fling the espresso into his face.

Then there was Hamish. Each time Lavinia

turned to Max for his opinion, Hamish stood rigidly still, his finger poised quizzically at the corner of his mouth. Mocking him, Max was sure. "And monsieur?" Hamish began to chime after Lavinia turned with yet another pillow or serving platter, adding yet another odious note to the absurd ritual. Max would have liked to flip him over and spin him round by the feet like a top on the highly waxed floor.

Now Hamish ran back toward Max, looking like a duck squeezed into an expensive suit. "Madame has gone off to call her place of work," he huffed. "She will meet you back here in five minutes."

Wordlessly Max dropped onto one of the large displays: a bed positively choked with veils, pillows, comforters, and throws. *Is this the kind of padding Lavinia's going to put on our bed?* Max thought, thinking with longing of his simple twin bed with the flat navy spread he'd had since he was nine, at Pennington House.

Hamish—who Max was convinced must be Scottish, despite his jaunty French accent—slowly bowed. "If you will excuse me, I will go inquire if madame would like to examine our very fine collection of teakwood as well," he said, keeping his head so low that Max could practically see his reflection in Hamish's shining pate.

Max waved him off without speaking, wishing he'd thought to bring a flask of something stronger than the beverage cart's tea with him as well.

The trip to Harrods had been a bone of contention right from the beginning of Max and Lavinia's engagement. At first Max had treated it like a joke he and Lavinia shared: a silly necessity that they would engage in merely out of formality, not because they truly desired a four-hundred-pound espresso maker and sixty-odd brandy snifters. "Perhaps we'll even give some of it to charity once we're out of the spotlight," Max remembered saying, and it seemed to him now that Lavinia had agreed.

But as the date for the wedding—and the due date for Max's thesis, which loomed even larger—drew nearer, Lavinia began to take the registry seriously—practically religiously. She would come home from work with names and suggestions from her long-married coworkers, which she dutifully entered into a leather-bound notebook that she consulted often. She began looking through high-end design magazines and dropping names like "Porthault" and "Limoges." And she arranged for a personal shopper to meet them at Harrods—meeting Max's shout of amusement with an icy hauteur and a slammed door.

"Lavinia, I do believe you've converted over to the enemy," Max had joked late one night over pasta at some incredibly overpriced bistro in Notting Hill. But his smile died on his lips as he caught a glimpse of Lavinia's steely gaze.

"Max, guests are going to be spending thousands of pounds on these gifts." Max had opened his mouth to retort, *Which is exactly why we shouldn't be swept up into this ludicrous situation!* but Lavinia lifted her hand to stop him, like a queen. "These are the things with which we're going to be starting our new lives together," she said, her clear blue eyes becoming glassy.

Max struggled for an answer. "I—I've just been concentrating on my thesis," he stammered.

Lavinia's voice was as sharp as the knife by her plate. "It doesn't seem to me that you've been working on your thesis at all," she said flatly. "It seems like you've been putting it off and putting it off." She cocked her head and looked at Max like he was a rare insect.

Max swallowed, trying to come up with a defense for the fact that he had barely completed ten pages in so many months. "I'm just looking at each section very seriously," he finally managed.

Lavinia's lower lip quivered. "Why can't you take this as seriously?" she asked, her voice sounding ragged at the edges.

Because I don't seriously believe we'll ever be married at all, Max's mind immediately replied. Although he hadn't spoken aloud, Max could see from the look on Lavinia's face that she had read his silence well enough. Stifling a sob, she threw down her napkin and ran into the bathroom, from where she emerged twenty minutes later, silent, her eyes red rimmed.

Max had spent the twenty minutes in agony, smiling nervously at the waiter to conceal the fact that anything was wrong, chewing rubbery ends of bread. He was shocked at the truth that Lavinia's tearful question had uncovered. Well, this sort of mucking about was no good. He was going to have to put this situation in order, no two ways about it. He set his elbows on the table like a general about to impart battle plans to his troops.

When Lavinia returned to the table, he was ready. As she sat down, looking away in anger, he took her hand. "Lavinia," he said. "I've been a jerk. Please forgive me. Get that whatever-his-name-is shopper to meet us, and I'll be there, with bells tied on."

Lavinia had turned to him, her joy and relief evident in the tears that finally spilled over her lashes, leaving two pale tracks on her ivory face. "Oh, Max, do you mean it?" she asked, sounding almost childlike in her delight.

"Of course," Max had said, setting his jaw so that his voice would sound hearty and determined, like the earl's did when he was making a declaration.

So that had been that—or at least, Max had thought that had been that. But it seemed that he couldn't make his "hearty determination" last through a morning with Hamish.

Suddenly Lavinia was in front of him, one lavender ballerina flat tapping impatiently. "Well, are you ready?" she said, as if she had been dragging Max around for hours.

She has, in a way, Max thought, giving up on mustering any enthusiasm. He could feel Hamish behind him: like a court jester, making faces when he wasn't looking. He glanced at his watch—good Lord, was it early afternoon already?

"Lavinia," he said, feeling like a heel even as he did it. "I promised Dad I'd hang out with Sarah this afternoon." *And thank God I did,* he refrained from adding.

Lavinia's eyes flashed, then became as dull as ice chips. "Fine," she said. "Hamish and I will be just ducky, won't we?" she cooed, briefly pressing Hamish's hand in her own.

If she thinks that's going to make me jealous, she's mad, Max thought, amused by the sight of Lavinia playing up to Hamish. For just a moment his mind

51

flashed to Elizabeth—he bet that she wouldn't tolerate that obsequious mallet head for one second. *Stop thinking about Elizabeth*, he chided himself. *You've got the woman you're supposed to focus on right in front of you.*

"Until later, then," Lavinia said, signaling to Hamish that they were dumping the grumpy fiancé.

"Wait!" Max cried, suddenly struck by a thought. He moved closer to Lavinia so that Hamish couldn't hear. "Listen, why don't you come by the house later?" he said, thinking of the conversation he'd had with the earl earlier about instructing Sarah in all the facts of life. Perhaps if he asked Lavinia to be the bearer of the birds and the bees, she would feel more involved with the family—and he with her.

Lavinia gave a little snort of laughter at Max's explanation. "I'm sure she'd rather shovel coal," she said, dismissing the idea with a wave of her hand. "If I can get Sarah to mutter 'fine' when I ask her what kind of day she's had, I think she's been bribed to do it."

Max's idea flattened slowly, like a balloon leaking air. Lavinia was right. Sarah would sooner join a nunnery than talk to Lavinia about sex.

"Well, see you later, then," Max said, leaning down to give Lavinia a perfunctory kiss on the cheek. Before he knew it, she had marched off, leaving a cloud of expensive perfume in her wake.

Suddenly Max realized who would be the perfect person to speak to Sarah. Someone intelligent, kind, and likable, but experienced—Max hoped—and distanced enough from the family that Sarah could speak to her without embarrassment.

Elizabeth Bennet.

Max snapped his fingers and set off for Pennington House to run his idea by the earl.

Having consumed three scones slathered with jam and clotted cream, James Leer pushed his plate away from him, feeling slightly queasy. He took a sip of tea, hastily blotting his mouth to keep from spitting out the entire mouthful all over his wool slacks. He picked up his copy of *The Economist*, flipped it open, then slammed it shut just as hastily. It was no use.

Vanessa, the maid at Pennington House, was indelibly stained on his brain, like an ink blot on a white shirt. Waving away the waitress, James settled his head in his hands and gazed at the passersby out the window, unable to concentrate on his thesis even for a minute.

This is ridiculous, James thought. *I'm all caught up in this terrible crush, and as it stands, I've hardly ever said two words to the girl.*

You've seen her, though, haven't you, his brain immediately responded. And in that moment James exited the café near the university where he had always enjoyed midmorning tea—at least before he had met Vanessa. Instead he was standing in the front hall of Pennington House, watching the beautiful ghost who had just taken his coat drift through the French doors.

James remembered not being able to speak. "Who in the world was that?" he asked, unable to take his eye off the spot Vanessa had just vacated, as if he watched it long enough, she would magically reappear there.

Max had looked at James with confusion, then great amusement. "Why, that's Vanessa," he had said, smiling broadly. "The newest addition to the household staff here at Pennington House."

Which is why she won't give me the time of day, James thought bitterly, swiping all of his sugar packets and plastic stirrers into a neat pile. He sighed and rolled his *Economist* up into his pocket. He was trying to signal the waitress for the check when a shadow fell across his table.

"James?" asked a soft, young, female voice.

James covered his eyes, as if shading them from the sun. For a moment he was convinced that the figure must be Vanessa—conjured up by the heat of his passion. It took the girl's stepping out of the

54

direct path of the sun to clear up the confusion.

"I thought it was you!" exclaimed a pleasant-looking, brown-haired girl. She sat down across from James, smiling widely. "You don't mind if I sit down for a moment, do you?"

James racked his brain for her name. He knew she was a fellow student and a recent one at that—was her name Katherine? Caitlin? "Katrin," he finally remembered, grasping her hand and pumping it enthusiastically, mostly out of relief at being able to dredge her name up from the gooey dregs of his Vanessa fantasies. "How are you doing?"

Katrin smiled and began to chatter. Evidently, James learned, after graduating she'd entered a Ph.D. program that combined history and economics at the University of London. She'd spent the past year in America doing research on the migration patterns of blacks during Reconstruction and the effects that had had on labor in Chicago and New York. *She's really blossomed since she was in school,* James thought, only half following, watching with unexpected pleasure as she pushed her sleek bob behind her ears. As Katrin told him about how addicted she'd become to something called IHOP pancakes while in America, her coffee-colored eyes flashed, and a slight dimple appeared in her left cheek whenever she smiled.

55

No wonder I didn't recognize her! James thought.

Still, his interest was more brotherly than romantic. Vanessa had eclipsed the space in his heart—there wasn't any room for passing fancies. Unfortunate, James decided, because Katrin—swinging her legs, smiling charmingly, looking like she had a fabulous secret each time she leaned down to sip her coffee—was certainly seeming very flirtatious. "So . . . ," Katrin said, finishing a long anecdote about finding some musty records in the bottom of an old Alabama city hall that was now used as a beauty parlor. "What have you been doing with yourself?"

James was amazed to find that he had nothing to respond with. *Dreaming about a beautiful maid,* he thought immediately, but of course he didn't voice his thoughts. "Just working on finishing my thesis," he finally threw out, trying to sound enthused about it, which he most decidedly was not.

Katrin's smile suddenly seemed a bit forced, James thought. "Weren't you working on that when I was in your class?" she said in a perky manner that reminded James of the one his mother used when she was asking if he had any female "friends."

James had to stop himself from flinging his computer over into the trash can and giving it all up right there. "Well, you can't order up a thesis like a pint of Guinness, can you?" he said, aware that he was practically baring his teeth in an effort to continue to smile politely.

Thankfully, Katrin laughed. "No, of course not!" she said. "I'm so stupid. I haven't even got my master's yet," she added.

And with that, James's self-confidence returned. "I'm sure you'll have it squared away in no time," he said generously.

"So, have you seen any good movies lately?" Katrin asked, smiling mischievously.

James knew this line—he recognized it as one he had used himself many times, with great success in the past, to get a girl to go out with him. And under any other circumstances, he would have been more than flattered to have Katrin use it on *him*.

But even though Katrin is exactly the girl my parents want me to have, James thought, *she's not the one I want to have.* Something further occurred to him. *She's the girl that I would think I would want to have too.*

But James knew he wanted another one.

"I haven't had any time for movies lately, unfortunately," James said. He felt instantly sorry when he saw Katrin's face fall at his cold response.

She recovered quickly, however. "Well, it's

57

been nice seeing you," Katrin said, giving James a genuine, wide, if slightly crestfallen smile. "I hope the thesis goes well."

She had picked up her coat and was prepared to leave when James stopped her. "Katrin, wait," he said. "I've got a friend who's doing a lot of work on the American South too—the Civil War. I'm sure he'd love to talk to you. Do you mind if I give him your number?"

Katrin's smile returned. Whether James's question had been a ruse or was a way of tardily flirting back, James could tell she didn't know yet, but luckily she had clearly forgiven him anyway. Smiling without reservation, she wrote down her number on a slip of paper and handed it across to him.

"Cheers," she said, waving, and with a tinkle of the door she was gone.

James looked down at the number, written in blue ink in delicate, sloping letters. *It's terrible,* James thought. *Just because the girl I like is out of line with the girls even I think I should like, my friend Grant gets this great girl's number.* He smiled, thinking of his lanky, handsome historian friend, who was currently single. He was sure that Grant and Katrin would hit it off.

Then he thought of Vanessa and her piercing dark eyes and black hair. Again he froze with longing.

But that's all right, James thought. *I'm satisfied with my lot.*

Max entered the empty hallway, silently uttering thanks that he wasn't greeted at the door by a sheaf of urgent messages from Lavinia or, worse, from Hamish. Feeling almost like a thief in his own home, he clutched his car keys in his pocket so they wouldn't jingle and started for the stairs.

"Mr. Max," Mary said from where she was standing, practically invisible, in the archway to the living room. Max nearly jumped out of his skin.

"Mary. Yes. What is it?" Max said, summoning his normal, relaxed visage as best he could after he had recovered from the shock.

Mary regarded him coolly, as if she could see how much Max wanted to get upstairs, safe and alone, free from any pillow shams or dust fans, or whatever they were called, as quickly as possible.

"You've a message," Mary said, her lined face giving away nothing.

Max sighed. *Here's where I hightail it back to Harrods,* he thought, already descending toward the foyer.

"Miss Sarah called to say she'll be a bit late," Mary continued, folding and refolding a cloth in her pocket. "Is that all right?"

Max tried to crush down the immediate rush of joy he felt at the news. "That will be just delightful, Mary," he said, bouncing upstairs to get away from the confused look she gave him.

Don't overanalyze this, Max, he told himself as he flopped on his bed briefly and checked his watch. Good. Just enough time to have a brief chat with the earl about his plan. *You just don't want to be sniffing out damask tablecloths and thread counts and whatnot, that's all. It's not that you don't love Lavinia.*

Max bounded up and headed to the earl's study, trying to avoid the nagging voice that said, *But if you love Lavinia, why are you so loath to get married to her? Shouldn't you be holding up a sheet and asking, Is this thread count 240 or 380?*

Max knocked on the earl's door. "Yes?" Max heard from inside, the earl sounding querulous and slightly irritated, as he always was when his private time in the library was interrupted.

Max poked his head in the door. "Dad? Can I speak to you a moment?"

The earl nodded, closing the book that he was reading and placing it on the side table. He stood and walked behind his desk, sitting behind the large chair, as if he and Max were about to have a formal interview.

Max smiled inwardly at the thought. *Hullo,*

Dad, I'm Max Pennington. I'm here about the job as a son?

Although his father was overly formal, Max couldn't blame him—wearing a floor-length robe and a powdered white wig gave one a certain air of gravitas in everyday matters. *No wonder Dad can hardly bear to speak about Sarah,* Max thought. *If only he could pass a measure in Parliament forbidding her to speak to boys!*

Max took his cue from his father and sat across from him. *Now, play this one close to the vest, Max,* he coached himself. *We don't want another one of these nasty little lectures from Pater on the "insupportability" of romances between servants and royals. I've got to seem completely disinterested in Elizabeth.* His mind turned over the "seem." *Which I am, of course,* he added.

"What would you like to speak about, Max?" the earl said dryly, since Max had been silently staring at the carved ashtray on his father's desk for about half a minute.

Max shook himself awake. *You've already made a mess of things this morning with Lavinia,* he thought. *Don't let Dad think you're incapable of handling the slightest task too.* "I had a thought regarding that, er, talk we had the other day," Max said, hoping he wouldn't have to get too specific again.

Max couldn't read his father's eyes. "What talk?" his father said, sounding only the smallest bit intrigued. The earl stroked the leather-bound Bible, the one that had been passed down in the family through hundreds of years, on his desk. "When?"

Max sighed. Clearly they were going to have to get into dodgy sex territory again—bollocks. "About Sarah, Father," Max said patiently. "Sarah's—er . . . growing up."

The earl's face reddened immediately, and he snapped his chair into an upright position. "Yes, yes, of course," he said hastily. "Did you have any, uh, further thoughts on that that you wished to share?"

Max would have smiled at the earl's discomfort if he hadn't felt so distinctly uncomfortable himself. "Yes, Father," Max said, relieved that this would soon be out of his hands. "I thought of someone who might just possibly serve to speak to her about . . . certain facts," he finished.

The earl, Max noted, looked terrified—almost as if he were afraid to hope lest Max disappoint him. *Father afraid!* Max thought with amusement. *And over this!*

"Lavinia thinks that her relationship with Sarah is insufficient—"

"Yes, yes," the earl said, as if he'd already

considered Lavinia and dismissed her. *Which perhaps he has,* Max thought abjectly. *But then again, it's not like sisters-in-law always become best friends.*

"The American maid," Max continued, careful not to use her name familiarly right from the outset. "The new maid, Elizabeth Bennet, is very personable. She might . . ."

Seeing the earl's face cloud over, Max let his voice peter out. It was hopeless. He'd really done it this time. The earl was going to accuse him of being smitten. Worse—obsessed. He'd have to sit through another lecture, perhaps many lectures. Perhaps Lavinia would even be told. And he knew that all it would do was stir up the feelings he was trying to hide in the first place.

Max wanted to bolt from the room before disaster struck.

"That might," the earl said, the first hint of enthusiasm creeping into his voice, "that might just do. . . ."

Why, he's not going to lecture me at all! Max thought. *He's as relieved to have someone to palm this off on as I am. More so, in fact . . .*

It was the perfect choice, after all, though, Max decided. Not only because he personally knew that Elizabeth was intelligent and caring—and clearly experienced with male attention, Max thought, thinking of her California good looks. *Her blue-green eyes* . . . he routed himself. She was outside the family. Now no one would have to actively deal with the embarrassment that was Sarah's burgeoning sexuality. "Son, you've done it," the earl said, coming around to Max and giving him a hearty clap on the shoulder. He took Max's hand and shook it heartily. "You'll do, you will. You'll do."

Despite himself Max blushed like a sixth former at the earl's praise.

Now that Sarah was taken care of, he only had to worry about Lavinia.

He hoped.

Chapter
Four

In the midst of preparation for tea Elizabeth and Cook were chopping up enormous piles of carrots, celery, and dill. (Cook had confided excitedly to Elizabeth some three times that she was going to show her "a proper leek soup—a proper leek soup!" a delicacy Elizabeth felt she could safely do without.) As Elizabeth hefted her cleaver, the intercom buzzed. Elizabeth brought the flat of the blade down on a head of garlic and reduced it to pulp, just as Cook had taught her—especially satisfying for those days when she couldn't stop thinking about Sam and Jessica. "Mary," Elizabeth heard the earl's voice intone. "Please send Miss Elizabeth Bennet to the study right away."

Elizabeth started, as did Cook, almost imperceptibly, and Alice across the room, who gave a little yelp, like a rabbit. "Yes, sir," Mary paged back right away, turning and giving Elizabeth a baleful look. Cook glanced at her, her large moon face ominous, then looked away quickly and resumed her energetic chopping. Alice simply made a terrified face, as if Death himself had come, with his sickle blade.

Elizabeth was as baffled as they were. Was this some kind of new-hire ritual? Could the earl be firing her?

Right, Elizabeth. Like the earl really takes the time to fire each servant personally.

Well, then, what was it? Elizabeth was surprised to realize that she felt as much trepidation as she had when she'd first received that thin envelope from the writing program at the University of London—the envelope that had led her on this cockeyed path in the first place. *That's ridiculous,* Elizabeth decided. *You can't mean that you're as invested in this job as you were in the idea of becoming a writer.*

Elizabeth raised her eyebrows at Mary, asking, *Am I excused?* without having to say the words. Somehow she was embarrassed—there were so many points of etiquette she didn't know, and this unscheduled meeting with the earl seemed another one. She'd never witnessed any earl–scullery-maid interviews in any of the Merchant-Ivory films.

"Yes, yes," Mary said, waving her on impatiently

and taking up her pen again with a fierce air of industry. That was so strange—Elizabeth could almost swear that Mary looked somewhat confused and discomfited too as Elizabeth took off her apron and hung it on the peg near the door.

Walking down the hall, she wondered what was in store for her. Was the earl going to lecture her about talking to Max in the garden? That couldn't be it. He'd surely just talk to Max, wouldn't he, and not bring the servants into it? Or use Mary.

Elizabeth gasped. Perhaps he'd found out that she wasn't really who she'd said. Perhaps there were police officers—Mounties? Bobbies?—waiting in the office right now, to take her away.

Except you haven't broken the law, Wakefield, Elizabeth told herself, trying to calm her pounding heart. *Unless getting a job under an assumed name and without a work permit is breaking the law. Even if it is, I'm sure the earl has better things to do with his time than research the appellations of his scullery maids.*

Reaching the earl's door, Elizabeth lifted her hand to knock, then hesitated. *Elizabeth, there are no boys in blue back there,* she told herself. *It's not like you left some trail of bodies in California, after all—you just wanted to leave things behind for a while.*

Suddenly Elizabeth had another thought—could

her *parents* have located *her?* Could they, in fact, be behind the door right now?

Elizabeth dismissed it, using her old journalistic skepticism to break down her worry step by step. She wasn't fourteen, after all—if any inquiry had come the house's way regarding her, Mary would have deflected it, saying that she could not reveal the parties working in the house except to the proper authorities. *The earl is a member of Parliament, you know, and as such must be protected by a certain amount of security,* Elizabeth could almost hear Mary saying crisply.

And if they'd come to the door, they would have been simply—turned away, Elizabeth realized. She pictured her parents, fitful, worried, heading back to some waiting taxi, unable to determine if their daughter truly was ensconced in the imposing castle. She didn't know how she felt about the image.

Suddenly the heavy oak door swung open from the inside, and the earl stood there, smiling broadly. Elizabeth could see that the sunny, oak-paneled library was completely empty. She had to fight the urge to apologize for all her panicky thoughts. *Wait and see,* Elizabeth thought. *Maybe he's just gone bonkers, and you're the first clue.*

Continuing to exhibit what, for him, was practically a large grin, the earl guided her inside and placed her in a small chair across from his desk.

He's smiling, Elizabeth thought, *so it can't be that bad, right?*

"Elizabeth, thank you for coming," the earl said, more volubly—and kindly—than she had ever seen him before. Normally the earl's series of faces was about as changeable as a line of scones on a baking tray. "I apologize for distracting you from your tasks, but I—perhaps—have a job for you. Please take a seat so we may discuss it."

God, English men are such smoothies, Elizabeth thought, marveling at the way that an accent and an adroit use of language could set one instantly at ease. Of course, that immediately brought to mind monosyllabic Sam, who had proved to be hiding plenty—like an affair with her sister—behind his silent veneer. *Who needs silence?* Elizabeth thought, trying to contain the rage brought on by the thought of Sam and Jessica. Elizabeth had gone almost a whole day yesterday without picturing the two of them in the hotel room, kissing, and she was frustrated by their aggressive reappearance in her thoughts. *Dammit, I'm not going to think about them anymore. I'll take this kind of smooth talker any day—as long as he's not hiding something too.*

The earl turned around, looking slightly befuddled himself. His brow was furrowed. He leaned against the edge of the desk. "Elizabeth, this is a delicate topic," the earl said, clasping his wrist with his hand and nervously—Elizabeth noticed—jiggling his watch with his thumb. "I hesitate to broach it with you, and I hope you will not take any offense."

Uh-oh, Elizabeth thought, drawing herself tighter into her chair. *This better not remind me at all of that hotel room, or I'm outta here faster than these Penningtons can clean out a platter of scalloped potatoes.* She wasn't all that worried, though—the earl didn't seem like the mistressy type. Unless you could consider a shelf of leather-bound books written entirely in Greek a "mistress."

"Miss Sarah," the earl began, then stopped. "It seems Miss Sarah," he continued, after a long pause, "has reached the age of adulthood."

At first all Elizabeth could think of was her father, when she and Jessica were twelve, taking them to the Sweet Valley Savings Bank to open up separate accounts and the thrill Jessica seemed to have gotten out of her own name typed across that tiny blue notebook, with the balance reading $50.00 beneath, followed by a row of periods.

I think the earl probably has Sarah's banking taken care of, Elizabeth thought, watching him screw up his patrician features in an effort to get the next words out. *And I imagine she has more than fifty dollars in her account too.*

Whatever this was, it had to be good if it was

making the earl uncomfortable. After waiting at table on the earl and his family, Elizabeth took a certain pleasure in watching him squirm. Still, she couldn't guess what he might be getting at. Something with school? Tutoring, perhaps? But it was unlikely that the earl would need to resort to his kitchen staff to get academic help for his daughter. Didn't they have tutors for that?

"Sarah has reached the age of . . . the age of . . ."

Watching the earl's face contort into something like a Pennsylvania funnel cake, Elizabeth suddenly understood what this must all be about. "I understand," she cut in smoothly, wanting to free the poor man of his agonies. It had all become clear. Sarah was a teenager, wasn't she? And she had no mother—or sister, aunt, or cousin, for that matter. And she was reaching the age when girls got involved with boys. The earl needed someone to talk to his daughter about . . . things.

And in the tiny world of Pennington House, she was his best bet.

It did make sense, Elizabeth realized. After you acknowledged the dearth of female relatives, there were only a couple of options. Max? Elizabeth had to stifle a laugh. The earl? Ha—he was barely able to say good morning to his children, much less explain the vagaries of love and sex. Mary Dale and Matilda Kippers, the cook, were of course too old and sexless—the earl would implode if he had to ask them for anything more than coffee. Vanessa—too mean. Alice—too flighty. So unless the earl wanted to import a sex counselor from London, Elizabeth—foreign, personable, and seeming experienced without seeming *too* experienced—must look like his only choice.

The earl looked terrified—as if Elizabeth might slap him and quit or—worse—go to the newspapers with the story. *Member of Parliament Needs Maid to Explain Birds and Bees*. Elizabeth tried to hide her smile, but it was pretty funny. She remembered vaguely that even her father had fled upstairs when her mother had explained what was going on in Judy Blume's *Are You There, God? It's Me, Margaret*.

"Unfortunately, Mrs. Pennington is deceased," the earl continued, adopting the sonorous, authoritative voice he used at Parliament, Elizabeth assumed, to hide his discomfort. "And there is no one—"

"Yes, I understand," Elizabeth said quickly, knowing she would laugh if the earl went on for too long. She had been so intimidated by the gleaming leather and low, expensive lamps of the office when she had walked in, feeling like a peasant among royalty. But this was an arena where the earl, clearly, wanted *her* to be in charge. So deferring to the help *was* acceptable, Elizabeth thought wryly, in certain situations.

Like when there was a really, really big mess you didn't want to clean up yourself.

Again Elizabeth saw herself and Jessica sitting across the kitchen table, gossiping about who was going to which dance with whom, and herself in her mother's lap, weeping incessantly about some fight with Todd, as she had countless times. She thought of endless trips to the beach with Todd and Jessica, Jessica watching new cute boys as if each was a Swatch she might want to purchase.

The thought that Sarah had no one but the maid to talk to suddenly made Elizabeth unaccountably sad.

Maybe it's because I'm just as alone as she is right now, Elizabeth thought, staring at the blisters on her palms.

"You do understand?" the earl said. "Because it has come to our attention at this time that Sarah has been—"

Elizabeth really didn't want to hear any aspects of Sarah's romantic life from the earl—that was bridging the employer-employee gap too handily for her. "I'll talk to her," she said again, trying to smile confidently. *There really is a big difference between the rich and everyone else,* Elizabeth thought. *Can you imagine if Mom had asked the maid—we didn't even have a maid!—to talk about sex with me and Jess? I'm sure the maid would have quit that crazy household right away.*

That brought up a new thought—perhaps she should refuse, out of the simple inappropriateness of the request? *But I like Sarah,* Elizabeth thought suddenly—surprised to find that she actually did. *And the earl doesn't seem like he'd fire me if I said no. He just seems like he'd be incredibly grateful if I said yes.*

The earl seemed still concerned, however. "So you will stress—ah—of course—the virtues of waiting, and—"

He has no idea how lucky he is to have stumbled upon me, Elizabeth thought, thinking grimly of all the times she'd almost lost her virginity in the past—then been so relieved, later, that she hadn't actually gone all the way. Still, Elizabeth had no intention of giving Sarah some unrealistic speech about sex that would go in one ear and out the other. "I'll do my best," she said, letting the earl take that whichever way he chose.

The earl seemed happy to believe that Elizabeth wouldn't wind up advising Sarah to cruise porn on the Internet and get a subscription to *Playgirl.* He turned around as if they had just completed a lucrative business deal and he was about to cut the deciding check. "Wonderful, then. Of course, you'll be compensated for your time and for your effort—"

Elizabeth had already risen to go, but she turned around. "That won't be necessary." *Being paid for giving advice to a teenager is too weird,* she thought. *Especially when her mother's dead.* But she had another thought. "But you understand I won't report back anything of what Sarah says," Elizabeth said, trying to sound polite. "I won't be a spy for you," she added.

As the earl shot Elizabeth a displeased glance, she quaked inside. *Where did that come from?* she thought, regretting her words. Still, she knew that she somehow had to make it clear—she would talk to Sarah about dating and boys for Sarah's benefit only—not for the earl's.

Even if it got her fired.

The earl looked like he'd just swallowed a bone with his fish. "Of course," he said clearly, but his face suggested that it wasn't acceptable, not at all. Elizabeth knew, though, that she had the upper hand. If they had turned to her, they understood that no one in the family—and perhaps on the rest of the staff—felt comfortable instructing Sarah in the birds and bees.

Oddly, Elizabeth did. The conversation had sparked such an onslaught, in fact, of memories of her own warm, familial, Jessica-filled adolescence that she was near tears. She needed to get to the bathroom. The loo. Whatever. Pronto.

"That—," the earl began, and Elizabeth could tell he was fighting against his usual "that will be all." "That will be very good, Miss Bennet." He smiled—an almost normal-size smile—this time. "And many thanks."

"Not at all," Elizabeth said, borrowing Mary's deferential reply to any thanks she received. Elizabeth even curtsied slightly as she left the room—some weird reflex from ballet when she was eight?

Noting that Max's car was in the driveway, Elizabeth made her way back to the kitchen. *Stop thinking about him, Elizabeth,* she cautioned herself. *Just concentrate on your writing.*

This job was becoming more personal than she had bargained for. And "personal" was exactly what she had come to England to escape.

Sarah ran one hand down the sleeve of Nick's maroon rugby shirt and smiled up at him—enigmatically, she hoped. An article in *Blush* magazine that she'd just read last night had said that half the key to keeping a guy in the palm of your hand was seeming mysterious. *And if I'm going to sort out how I really feel about sex in time for tomorrow,* Sarah thought, *I'd better be the bleeding Mona Lisa.*

Nick grinned and pressed Sarah closer, running his large hand up and down her back—*a singular place for a man's hand to be,* Sarah recited to herself silently, remembering Catherine Sloper, the heroine of Henry James's *Washington Square,* from when they had read the book last quarter in English class. *Thank God I have Nick,* Sarah thought, *and I'm in no danger of getting thrown over and having to needlepoint my entire life.* Nick's fingernails brushed her spine. *At least, I better not be,* she amended.

"I'm thinking," Sarah said playfully, and returned his kiss, rising up slightly on the tips of her toes to reach Nick's nose.

As usual, after Latin she and Nick had brushed off their classmates and found an empty classroom to snog in. Their favorite was the wood-paneled senior English room, the one shaped like an L, so that it was impossible for anyone walking by the door to look in and see Nick and Sarah doing what they were decidedly not supposed to be doing.

And no one better catch us, Sarah thought, looking with anxiety toward the huge oak door. *If I get pulled in to see the headmistress again, I'm out for sure.*

Sarah shivered and hopped up on a nearby desk so that she could wind her arms around Nick's back and gaze at him face-to-face, adoringly—the way girls always snogged guys in the movies. This position also afforded her a better view of the door, which had begun, in Sarah's eyes, to loom amazingly large, like a door in the scene of a TV

77

show that you *knew* had to be opened once or twice by some character or it wouldn't be in the shot at all.

Dad's made me into a nervous maniac! Sarah thought with discomfort.

She tried to forget her fears by diving in for some more snogging. But Nick, ever vigilant, leaned back and continued to look at Sarah searchingly, only lightly running his palms up and down the sleeves of her turtleneck. It didn't matter—Nick's touch was enough to keep Sarah feeling permanently depleted of oxygen.

"Thinking about what, love?" Nick said.

Sarah sighed happily. She loved it when Nick called her "love"—it was like they were already an old married couple sitting together in a pub or something. Each time he prefaced a sentence with "love," or "darling," or even "Sare," she felt some invisible addition had been made to the tally of their growing love for each other.

Also, frankly, a term of endearment was a term of endearment.

"Tonight," Sarah said, and tried to smile happily so that Nick wouldn't realize how worried she actually was about accomplishing their secret plan—to sneak off to one of Nick's favorite local pubs.

"Oh," Nick said, drawing the word out softly. He traced her nose with his finger, then leaned in

for a really, really deep snog. Fireworks erupted, making Sarah's scalp tickle. It felt, Sarah thought, like her tongue had been plugged into an outlet that led directly to permanent bliss.

Evidently Nick felt the same. After they kissed, he leaned down and put his head into the curve of her neck. "You're the greatest," he murmured, nibbling slightly at the fleshy lobe of her ear.

"Oh, Nick!" Sarah giggled. "That tickles!" Actually, she didn't want him ever to stop, but the *Blush* article had also said that resistance was the path to always getting what you wanted.

But what is it that I want? Sarah asked herself. *Well, except to keep snogging Nick forever.*

It seemed to Sarah sometimes that she and Nick had stumbled upon some completely secret world that no other adult could possibly understand. For instance, her dad. *I mean,* Sarah thought, *I can barely picture him in his knickers—ugh—much less kissing Mum—or anyone—like this. And Max and Lavinia? Ha! I bet all they do every time Max goes over there is wind up sitting in some dark room in that huge old house of hers, with* Antiques Roadshow *on the telly, playing endless games of whist.*

Did all adults know about sex? How wonderful it felt to kiss each other on the nose and simply stand around, holding hands? *They couldn't,* Sarah thought, *or nothing would get done. They'd all be squirreled away like me and Nick, snogging all day long.*

Or doing more, Sarah thought miserably, unable to keep her anxiety about tomorrow night from returning again and again to her thoughts. Nick had graduated from her ears to her neck and was now slowly kissing the portion that ran from her ear to her collarbone. She felt her breathing become more husky, like she was the woman in the sex scene in some movie, and was both thrilled and terrified. One part of her wanted nothing more than to disappear with Nick into his bedroom and emerge a woman, whatever the consequences. And the other part of her felt that losing her virginity would be as ludicrous as suddenly standing up, slapping on a wig, and giving a speech in Parliament.

But women don't wear those wigs! Sarah thought, trying to banish the worry that was giving rise to these ludicrous thoughts. *Oh, I wish I had someone to talk about Nick with,* she thought suddenly, surprising herself. *Victoria's still a virgin, Lavinia—ugh—probably thinks sex would ruin her nails, and Max would run out of the room screaming if I so much as uttered the dreaded S word in his presence.*

"You're a peach, darling," Nick murmured, the new term making Sarah feel like she'd just drunk a shot of very spiked punch. *Peach!* Nick must really love her. Slowly Nick let his hand drift from her knee toward her upper thigh. Despite herself Sarah put out a hand to stop him—catching it with her own, as if she'd only been desperate to hold hands. Nick didn't seem deterred and merely put his other hand into use. Sarah slid her own hand just as nonchalantly down to prevent it from going any higher. *See, I need someone who can tell me how to handle this situation,* she thought, grabbing both of Nick's hands and forcing them behind her back, as if she was merely hungry for a closer embrace.

"Oh, darling, I can't wait until tomorrow," Nick said, his kisses increasing in urgency. For a moment Sarah thought he meant that he'd like to do it *right there*—her heart leaped into her throat—then realized he merely meant that he was looking forward to their assignation, a lot.

Sarah tried to show him that she couldn't either, kissing him more deeply, occasionally mashing her teeth against his gums in their mutual ardor. *Someone who could show me how to kiss without giving the man a tooth cleaning,* Sarah thought. "Me too," she whispered, although what she really wanted to say was, *I can. How do you put a man off without making him stop liking you?* she asked herself. What was she going to do? She couldn't very well drift into Nick's bedroom like she was all ready to get hot and heavy, then distract him with a game of backgammon.

Or could she?

But this afternoon was another story. Sarah and Nick were going to head over to a local pub—a real "man's" pub, Nick had said—and meet some of his friends. *That* Sarah really couldn't wait for. Even though Sarah, of course, couldn't invite Nick for dinner and have her father look him over—*All Dad would want to do is call Victoria's dad and have him send Nick to Zimbabwe*—he wasn't holding it against her. He was drawing her closer into every aspect of his life, trying to make her a part of it. Suddenly Sarah had a thought. Maybe she could talk to Elizabeth, that new American maid, about all this dating stuff. American girls were knowledgeable about that kind of thing—weren't they? They certainly seemed like all they did was date in their TV shows and movies. *But I'm already using Elizabeth to get Max in trouble,* Sarah thought with irritation. *I can't very well build up Max's crush, then ask her about sex. She'll put the wrong two and two together.*

Sarah thought with pleasure of her long-term scheme to throw Max and Elizabeth together and how the earl—apoplectic with rage over Max's mooning over an American maid—would be far, far too distracted to worry about her and Nick.

And if I keep flirting with James so convincingly, Nick and I will be able to do more of this all day, Sarah thought, nearly squirming with pleasure.

Anyway, that maid's too goody-goody to give me any decent advice, Sarah told herself. *If she had any interest in sex, she'd be off snogging Max somewhere, not burrowing away at that stupid journal in the garden all the time.*

Sarah had had enough of thinking about her stupid, robotic adult guardians and how absolutely useless they all were to her. She concentrated instead on kissing Nick back—trying to use that new whirl-around kiss technique she'd read about in *Jump* magazine.

"So you'll meet me at the usual place at three?" Nick said, finally pulling out of the embrace long enough to catch his breath.

Sarah stroked the black curls around his ear. "Of course," she said, thinking about how she was going to get out of her afternoon plans of attending a play with Max. What would be best? To be sick? Depressed? Bogged down with schoolwork?

"And don't worry about anything," Nick said.

Sarah laughed. "I'm not worried, Nick," she said, trying to sound sophisticated. She *wasn't* worried, though, so it wasn't that hard to seem confident. "I've been to pubs before, you know!"

Nick's face grew very serious, then broke into a

smile. "I wasn't thinking about today," he said. To Sarah, he looked almost drunk—*drunk with love,* she thought happily. He leaned in close to her ear. "I was thinking about *tomorrow,*" he whispered.

Sarah shivered again. "Oh," she said. *Don't worry . . . meaning?*

"I've got *lots* of protection," Nick whispered.

Suddenly Sarah wanted Nick away from her ear and as far away from her as possible. What was wrong with her? To cover her feelings, she jumped up and put on her coat. "I've got to get back home," she said. "To cover my tracks, you know."

From three feet away Nick suddenly looked as cute again as he always had. *Protection* echoed in Sarah's mind. *Protection.* From Nick? But he was just the same Nick she'd known, not some scary incubus. *Protection* made everything sound terribly dirty, however, and much more like an AIDS ad on the Tube than the dreamy movie romance Sarah had been thinking of moments before.

Nick leaned in to kiss her, and Sarah felt terribly grown-up as their lips met, but in a pleasant way this time. It was like she was leaving for work at the door to the flat they shared together or something.

"See you soon," Nick said. Sarah arched her neck away so his words wouldn't come anywhere near her ear again.

"See you soon," Sarah echoed, trying to sound like the ladies in adverts, going off to bring home the bacon. She tripped out into the halls and then through the main doors into the cold, sunny day.

What if we really were married? Sarah thought, the idea rising through her flesh like yeast through dough. She felt hot and cold at the same time. The sun seemed unbearably bright after the dark, exciting classroom, and she yearned to be back in a car speeding toward home.

What had happened to make her want to get away from Nick so suddenly?

By the time Sarah slipped into Pennington House, it felt like it was the middle of the night instead of early afternoon. *Well, that's what snogging all day will do for you,* Sarah thought. *Another reason why I can't believe that any adult I know has ever done it—ever.*

Climbing up the steps to her bedroom, she yawned deeply. "I *am* kind of sleepy," she said to herself, glad to reach her four-poster bed swathed in a rich, thick down comforter. "Just lie down for a minute," she murmured, hugging a pillow and kissing it, as if Nick's face were stamped on the crisp cotton.

The next thing Sarah knew, she was side by side with Mum, riding Swift and little Butter, the gentle little pony that Mum had arranged to keep stabled at the house with Swift so that Sarah could learn to ride as well, when she was six years old. Mum leaned over and smiled at Sarah, winking a little bit, as if to say, *Isn't this grand?*

Mum! Sarah wanted to cry out in her sleep. *I've got so many things I need to ask you!*

But little dream Sarah did no such thing. She simply grinned at her mother and urged Butter into a canter, to keep up with Swift.

Sarah realized she was standing on the outside, looking in on her mother and the young girl, as if they were photos in a frame—or she was. *Mum!* Sarah cried loudly. *Mum! Wait for me!*

Her mum and her younger self looked back at her, smiling. But they continued cantering, far across the fields, farther and farther from Sarah with every passing second.

And she couldn't run after them. A great hand was reaching out from somewhere, pulling her back as she tried to go forward.

"Mum!" Sarah was groaning into her pillow. "Mum!"

Someone was shaking her, she realized. She turned over sleepily, a headache splitting her skull like a crack in a stone.

Max was leaning over her, looking at her worriedly. "Sarah?" he asked, holding a cool hand to her forehead. "Are you ill?"

Suddenly Sarah remembered where she was.

She was in her bed, at home, and she was sixteen. Butter and Swift were long gone, sold off and pastured years ago.

And so is Mum, Sarah thought, feeling a sudden welling up of sadness.

Sarah looked at Max, his face prompting a desperate fear she couldn't name. "Oh, Max!" she cried suddenly. She buried her head in his shoulder and burst into a quick storm of tears.

Max stroked her back stiffly—perplexed, she could tell. She couldn't remember the last time she'd hugged her brother—even punched him on the arm. They weren't, she thought, a demonstrative family, the sobs suddenly drying up almost as quickly as they'd come, like storm clouds.

"Sorry," she said, drawing back and reaching to her night table for a Kleenex. "I had a bad dream, that's all."

Suddenly Sarah remembered Nick and their plans. The thought of the pub and Nick's arm around her blew the last vestiges of the sadness away. She almost grinned until a thought struck her. *Oh, no! Now Max will be worried and insist that I come to the play to cheer me up.* She groaned inwardly.

"Are you sure you're all right?" Max said, still looking worried but also mildly uncomfortable, as if now that Sarah had cried, she might also grow another head or something.

Sarah tried to think quickly. "I think I'm coming down with something," she said, just as Max broke in with, "You look a little sick."

Max laughed lightly. "You'd better stay in bed," he said. "We'll just forget the play for today."

Sorted! thought Sarah gleefully. She tried to hide her delight. Now that she was fully awake, she felt rested and ready to roll out with Nick. But she had to make sure Max didn't see that.

Sarah sank back on the bed a little dramatically, reaching for another Kleenex to hide her smile. "But what about the play?" she asked, trying to keep her voice whispery and frail, like she had consumption.

Max stood up, looking a little leery. "I'll just take Lavinia," he said, as if he'd now be forced to drink Borox the rest of his life instead of water.

Max's resigned antipathy made Sarah want to scream. *Why are you marrying the girl if you don't even want to go with her to a play!* she restrained herself from shrieking in exasperation.

"I'm going to send Mary in to look after you," Max said. He appeared to think it over and shifted back and forth on the carpet. "Or would you like me to stay and bring you some tea and magazines?"

As much as Sarah enjoyed hanging out with her older brother, she had no intention of missing an evening with Nick. *Anyway, how much of that, dear brother,* Sarah wanted to ask, *comes out of concern for my health, and how much out of a desire to avoid Lavinia?*

But Sarah hadn't been Max's sister all these years for nothing. "Oh, I just want to sleep," she said, uttering a fake yawn.

Max sighed deeply—more pained by his sudden fate, Sarah knew, than he would have been by any illness. "All right," he said reluctantly.

Sarah suddenly had a brainstorm. "Elizabeth was looking for you earlier," she said. That should keep Max occupied for a while.

Max's face lit up. "Elizabeth? The maid?" he asked, not even noticing how obviously soppy he'd just gotten.

"Yes," Sarah said, trying to keep her voice entirely neutral.

Max began to whistle and stood, all of his good cheer returned. "Sleep well," he said, leaning over to pull Sarah's sheets up to her chin.

Sarah turned over and put her cheek to the cool pillow. Suddenly she felt Max's lips lightly brush her forehead, and then he was gone.

Sarah looked up at the ceiling, smiling. Now she would have time to get dressed and escape while Max went off to find Elizabeth and dither with her in the garden. And Sarah could call

Victoria and forget the fact that she'd been thinking so much about her mother lately.

And how much of that kiss, Sarah wondered, *was out of concern for my sickness, and how much was for mentioning Elizabeth Bennet?*

Chapter Five

Max halfway skipped down the hallway from Sarah's room, whistling to himself, until he caught a glimpse of his face in one of the floor-to-ceiling mirrors lining the hallway. Good God—he was grinning like a *perfect idiot*. Had Sarah noticed anything? Max thought of her greenish, flushed face, how she had clung to him and wept. So strange—Sarah never cried. But then again, she rarely got sick. *And what kind of a bloke are you anyway,* he chastened himself, *worrying about your stupid crush being unmasked while your sister is practically on her deathbed?*

This Elizabeth Bennet crush was slowly slipping out of control, Max decided, if he was running goofily around the halls like some kind of sixteen-year-old prom queen. Perhaps his father had a point.

The essential thing, Max thought, *is that Lavinia cannot find out.* For some reason, he thought of Lavinia's perfectly manicured nails—arched half-moons. It was ridiculous, but their severe regularity seemed to sum up everything about their relationship: a tidy, structured ideal that he must uphold at any cost.

Nope, he thought. *You just can't argue with nails like that.*

Still, it was undeniable that the fact that Elizabeth had asked—actually *asked*—for him was now causing a riotous uproar in his system. Standing before the mirror that led down the large, curving, central stairway, he brushed his hair out of his eyes and straightened his collar. *Shipshape, my man,* he told himself. *That's right. Pull yourself together. All systems go.*

Max headed down the stairs, pulling the tickets out of his pocket and looking them over. They were for a new play by a playwright he greatly admired—a young Irishman who had taken London by storm with his last work, *Medusa in Dublin,* an autobiographical retelling, it was said, of his parents' marriage. When it had come out, Max had gotten tickets and taken Sarah for her birthday. For nearly three hours he had sat in the theater with his sister at his side, blown away by the passion, the remarkable *incisiveness,* of the story—how, through the smallest of words and gestures, the playwright had somehow gotten across all the joys, the terrors, the sadness of marriage.

The institution he was about to embark on himself, Max thought.

Max fumbled in his pocket for his cell phone. *I should really call Lavinia now,* he thought. *Before she buys out half of Harrods.*

But somehow Max couldn't bring himself to. Instead he was picturing mile-high stacks of china, endless bolts of linen, crystal and silverware strewn in weighty piles across the floor of his bedroom, like a dragon's lair.

Max's finger hesitated over the sleek buttons. *Just do it, man,* he urged himself. *Hell! You're just inviting your fiancée to a simple date, that's all. Because your sister canceled on you! You go places with Lavinia all the time! It's not that complicated!*

But was it? When Max tried to push the buttons, he felt like a ten-thousand-pound weight was centered over his chest. He could barely breathe.

If he dialed Lavinia's number, the weight might fall and crush him completely.

I'll just see what Miss Bennet needed first, Max decided, sticking the phone back in his pocket and heading back down the stairs. *Then I'll call Lavinia and go fetch her. There's plenty of time.*

But how . . . ah . . . er . . . how, exactly, was he

going to locate Miss Bennet without alerting the household staff?

Since she had entered the Pennington household, Max had depended on regular mealtimes to see Elizabeth, or he had simply run into her in the garden, when she was working on her journal. *Which is exactly what I should be doing with my thesis,* Max thought, as usual feeling an uncomfortable tug at his gut at the thought of finally handing it in.

From time to time Max also caught her in a hall or speeding around on some task out in the herb garden, but there was certainly no "Bennet" schedule he could consult for such things. Mary? He couldn't ask her—it would look decidedly strange. Cook? Certainly not; he barely knew the woman. One of the other maids, like Vanessa or Alice? Well, first of all, he wasn't any more likely to come across them wandering around the house randomly than he was to happen upon Elizabeth. And second, even if he did, telling that sharp-tongued Vanessa or that giggly Alice anything seemed like an invitation to set off a bomb of gossip and intrigue in the servants' quarters—the *last* thing he wanted to do.

This is ridiculous, Max thought. *I'm sitting here plotting on how to get the attention of a servant . . . in my own house!*

Max suddenly chafed at the position he was in. *Because I* don't *really think of Elizabeth as a servant,* he thought slowly. *I don't think of her as being different from me . . . or from Lavinia, for that matter.*

Max walked over to the large grand piano in the main parlor and began to idly pluck out some Chopin. *That's the whole problem with this whole bloody lord-commoner business,* he thought. *It's a holdover from medieval times—and I don't believe in it at all. Dad does, though. Dad is depending on me to hold up the entire castle on my shoulders— powdered wig and knee breeches and all.*

Max suddenly hit a dissonant chord and brought his finger up to the smooth enamel to stroke it. As a child, he had never been able to keep himself from leaving fingerprints all over it, even though he only liked touching it because it was so smooth and shiny. The piano was dusted and polished every day—perhaps by Elizabeth, in fact. *Lavinia,* he thought, thinking back to his responsibilities, *Lavinia believes in it. And she expects me to believe in it too—when sometimes, now, I think, I'd like to chuck the whole bloody mess.*

The thought was so anarchic and unexpected that Max actually laughed out loud. *Chuck it . . . for what?* he thought, forcing another half laugh out of his dry throat. It sounded more like a cough. *A flat in London? A job at a newspaper? Coming home and making goulash for dinner on my hot plate with . . . Elizabeth Bennet?*

Max had only conjured up the tidy domestic scene to convince himself of the absurdity of the fantasy. But something else happened when he thought of giving up Pennington House, Lavinia, and his father's seat in Parliament. The image of him and Elizabeth crowded into a tiny flat only seemed . . . pretty damn great.

Max brought his hand to his forehead. *Perhaps I would,* he thought. *Perhaps I might like that kind of a life . . . at that.*

He laughed aloud again, trying to push the dizzying thoughts aside. *Don't be stupid, Max,* he cautioned himself. *People don't simply throw over their entire lives—their whole history, everything they've been working for since they were practically born—for a stupid girl.*

Except Elizabeth's not a stupid girl, Max thought. *She's a great girl—a fabulous girl—and I can't stop thinking about her.*

Despite himself Max couldn't help thinking of the most famous of all English romances: not Diana and Prince Charles—*Lord, no,* Max thought—but instead Edward VII and Wallis Simpson, the American divorcée who he had given up the crown for.

There's a man who gave up far more than I

would for Elizabeth—and publicly too, Max thought, horrified but also strangely exhilarated by the rising tide of thoughts. *And Elizabeth's not even a divorcée.*

It was too much. "I've got to get out of here," Max announced, standing up and pulling down the piano lid with a loud bang. *I've got to get out of here,* his thoughts repeated. *Get out of here and work, concentrate on real things. Sort things out.*

Pushing his hands into his pockets, Max strode down the hallway toward the sunporch. He flung open the door and rushed out into the sunlight, taking deep breaths as if he had been underwater for the past ten minutes. *Now, just take a seat in the garden. Then you can call Lavinia.*

The thought caused the dread to rise in his throat again, but Max choked it down, talking to himself as if he were a high-strung horse that was about to buck.

That's right, mate. Keep it slow. Slow and easy.

Out of the corner of his eye Max suddenly saw a flash of gold. He turned around. Elizabeth's ponytail flipped out of sight and disappeared down the stone steps into the kitchen.

Max had to fight himself to keep from shouting out after her. But he couldn't—everyone else in the kitchen would hear too, wouldn't they? And what would they think if the son of the house was

97

running around shouting after one of the maids?

Frowning, Max flipped open his cell phone again and hit the speed dial that connected him to Lavinia. As the number of rings increased, Max's frown grew deeper. Finally Lavinia's cool, collected voice ushered from her voice mail. Where was she? Max flipped the phone closed, removed the tickets from his pockets, then ripped them in half and let them flutter to the grass.

You've got a big, big problem, mate, he told himself.

He knew the girl he wanted to ask to the play wasn't Lavinia.

It was Elizabeth Bennet.

Vanessa slipped down the hallway toward the earl's home office, a feather duster held rigidly aloft in her left hand.

The coast was completely clear. The earl had left for work shortly after a light lunch in his office. Max was off with his new laptop, working on his thesis in the gardens (and more than likely, Vanessa thought, hoping to catch a glance of Elizabeth as he pored over whatever grand historical theories he was mucking about with). Mary and Alice had driven off to town to buy supplies for tomorrow's fancy fiancée dinner. Vanessa smirked. *If Lavinia finds out about her soon-to-be hubby's little crush on the help,* she thought, *we'll be eating him for dinner, not Mary's standing rib roast.*

Elizabeth was also safely tucked away in some other corner of the gardens—that was, if she hadn't settled herself right in with Max too. *I wish those two would just run off and get it over with,* Vanessa thought grumpily. *Everyone would be so distracted, I'd have some time to really search this idiotic house properly.* Another thought occurred to her: *The earl would already be so traumatized,* she thought, *I would have no problem about just asking him straight off if he's my father.*

Vanessa hesitated momentarily before the earl's massive office door. *Why am I being such a coward? Why don't I just ask him right now anyway?* she thought.

The scenario unfolded in Vanessa's head. Tomorrow night, in the middle of dinner, she would spoon gravy onto the earl's plate, then simply continue standing there. When he finally noticed, she would avert her eyes from his questioning glance. And when he finally spoke, she would answer whatever earl-like "That will be all" issued from his horrid mouth with an equally firm, *"No, Father, that will not be all. That will not be all at all."*

And I'll sound like a bloody goose, Vanessa

thought, laughing despite herself. She opened the door and strode in as if the office was hers. *I don't want a big dramatic scene. They'll just call the police and cart me off in a lorry. I want evidence—hard evidence—so that the earl can't squirm out of it whatever he does.*

Like he's been doing for the past twenty-odd years.

Vanessa had already searched this room twice, so she knew that the hard, ridged interiors of all the books yielded nothing. (And she wasn't going to search through the complete sets of Dickens, Thackeray, and Shakespeare with a fine-tooth comb while teetering on a wooden ladder ever again, thank you very much.) The same went for the large cabinets below the west-facing windows. Strangely, they were almost completely empty, except for a few pens, Parliament transcripts, and other oddments.

But she'd always been too afraid to search what she was sure would hold the most important information: the massive, gleaming desk in the center of the room.

All right, darling, she thought, as if she were talking to a very large tiger. *This won't hurt at all. . . .*

Pricking her ears for any sounds in the hall, Vanessa dropped to her knees and began to rifle through the contents. The main central drawer held exactly what you'd expect: rubber bands, pens, blotting paper, paper clips. The framing drawers were equally fruitless—one was filled with blank calling cards, the other with thick, creamy paper—*For the earl's brilliant thoughts,* Vanessa thought. *Of course, he can't just use stickies like everyone else.*

The bottom drawer, however, yielded a stunning photo so quickly, Vanessa was almost afraid she was imagining it. Jammed in a box with odd shots of Max, Sarah, and the former Mrs. Pennington, there was a lone black-and-white shot of her own mother. She was standing with a considerably younger earl, who was wearing what looked like tennis clothes. He had his arm casually thrown around her shoulders.

Vanessa gasped, then immediately burst into tears. Validation had come, but she hadn't known how painful it was going to feel. All this time now she had been stoking herself on rage: rage at the earl's incredible wealth, rage at his complete indifference to her, rage at the thought of her mother, drunk and utterly used up by life.

Now Vanessa was feeling rage *and* sadness. No: *sadness* was too small a word. It was an incredible, searing, inchoate grief at this picture of her mother—so small, so delicate, so innocent. So completely different than any woman Vanessa had ever known.

Vanessa covered her eyes quickly, afraid to look again. She peeked through her fingers. There she was again—her mother, half her face covered in shadow, waving to whoever was taking the photo. *Mum!* Vanessa wanted to yell across the decades at the image. *I'm finally here! I'm going to set things right in this house—finally.*

She had never realized her mother had once been so pretty. So—beautiful.

There was a loud bang in the hall. Vanessa jumped up like a shot, crushing the picture back in with all the others. Moving the feather duster back and forth, she made her way toward the door, finally relaxing once she had her hand on the knob.

She pulled it open. No one was there.

Farther down the hall a shutter banged again. Vanessa sighed and walked toward it, securing it with its latch as fiercely as she had sometimes seen parents plunk their errant children back into their seats on the Tube.

She walked down the hall toward the door again. Somehow, though, she couldn't enter it. It wasn't only that time had passed and Mary and Alice might be searching about for her any minute. It was that she had been *right*.

As much as she'd oriented her entire life around finding out the true secret of her past and bringing all the wrongdoers to justice, she—she now realized—had never thought that she'd actually be able to find the proof she needed. She had thought, Vanessa mused, that she would waste her life away trying to get the earl to admit what had happened, be eaten up by rage, hatred, and poverty, and die a bitter old woman.

Well, now that didn't have to happen. She could sneak back and get the photo tonight and do whatever she wanted with it. She could blackmail the earl. She could send it to the papers. She could send it to *Parliament*.

Would that silly, moony James Leer feel better about her once he knew she was royalty too?

Now, what did I think that for? Vanessa wondered. Normally she thought of James as a minor nuisance—although his devotion to her was kind of sweet. *Although who knows if it's really devotion?* Vanessa's rougher side cut in. *He probably wants to just use me and forget me, like the earl did to my mother.*

No, this photo was the most important thing in Vanessa's life right now—boys couldn't be trusted; they weren't worth anything. She'd seen enough of that her entire life to stay happily single forever.

But the photo . . . the photo was going to leave its sheltered life in that drawer very soon, Vanessa thought.

*　　*　　*

Elizabeth slowly walked down the kitchen steps, leaning over to sniff the fresh herbs—chives, rosemary, thyme—she had just plucked, well, neatly snipped, actually, straight from the garden. It was all she could do to refrain from humming a few bars from that old Simon and Garfunkel song, "Scarborough Fair." She would have liked it if the herb garden had brought back memories of a childhood spent running through cultivated gardens like these in a white flowing dress, but in fact it only brought back memories of . . . the vegetable aisle in a supermarket. *So much for my sunny, outdoorsy California upbringing,* Elizabeth thought.

As she plunked the straw basket (a real straw basket! *It would probably cost two hundred dollars in any American gardening catalog,* Elizabeth thought wryly) down on the central table, Cook swooped in and instantly plunged the herbs into a stream of hot water. "We could use some more fast workers like 'Lizbeth round 'ere," Cook said, glaring balefully at Alice, who merely ducked her head and resumed stirring whatever sauce she was allowing to thicken.

Elizabeth began to fill some prefluted (but homemade, of course) mini–pie crusts with a strawberry filling, as she had been instructed to do before Cook remembered she needed some more herbs from the garden. As usual, the repetition—dip, lift, scoop out, repeat—was calming instead of mind numbing. Since she'd taken this job, she'd used all the tasks as a kind of therapy. If she cleaned the grate properly, Sam and Jessica hadn't kissed (maybe didn't exist); if she made sure each windowsill was completely free of dust, her parents hadn't completely abandoned her to her sister's capricious will.

But I wonder how long that's *going to last,* Elizabeth thought. *I can't shake out sheets and smooth duvets forever.*

With each spoonful, Jessica and Sam—and her life with those two cheating, lying losers, she added angrily—were seeming further and further away, like the motorcycle crash she'd been in during high school, she thought. *Soon it'll be almost as if that all happened to another Elizabeth,* she told herself, wiping some extra strawberry goop onto her apron. (Cook was rabid about any surreptitious licking of any fingers or other body parts during cooking.) *In fact, it's starting to seem like that already.*

However, something else was coming in to fill their places in her brain. And Elizabeth knew exactly who that something was.

God, Elizabeth, get over it, will you? she told herself for the nine-hundredth time, glancing up at the steam-covered basement window as if she could will Max's feet and trousers to appear there immediately.

It's not like you haven't been clued in to the fact that he's about to get married, you know, Elizabeth thought, switching to the next tray of minipies while she rapidly lectured herself. *Where did he go last night, as usual? What special menu have we been discussing for the last eight hundred days? Who is coming to dinner tomorrow to eat these pies?*

Trying to stifle a wish for a full-size pie to shove in the smug (Elizabeth was sure) Lavinia's face, Elizabeth hoisted the tray over one shoulder and deposited it neatly into the enormous, walk-in freezer. She repressed the urge to lower her forehead against the cool, misting walls. *That's all you need, Elizabeth—to be stuck to the wall of this freezer for an hour or two while everyone wonders where you are—then comes and finds you hanging out like a human-size Popsicle.*

Deftly hoisting the second tray and sliding it into place, Elizabeth walked over to the counter and continued the lecture. *It's fine if you just want to have a little crush to get your mind off Sam, you know,* she thought. *You just have to make sure you remember that nothing—nothing!—is ever going to happen between you. Nothing. He's not any closer to noticing you for real than Prince William is.*

Despite herself Elizabeth's thoughts returned to their chats in the garden—Max strolling over slowly, then plunking himself at her side and initiating the kind of getting-to-know-you chat she hadn't had since she was at SVU, where random people squirreled in close to other students and got to know them all the time.

But it's not the same, Elizabeth! she practically yelled aloud, looking up in fright to see if anyone had noticed her look of frustration. She was hurriedly skinning the pot of potatoes Cook had placed in front of her. *Oh, Cook's so in love with your work lately, she probably would just think you were comparing your scraping of one potato to some perfect abstraction,* she thought.

But Max. Remember, Max hasn't met many Americans. He's just being friendly, like a lord of the manor. Talking to the help to show how open-minded he is. Making sure he doesn't become as bone-dry as his father.

Elizabeth stopped peeling momentarily and felt her collarbone. She felt warm. *It's Max,* she realized, reddening. *It's just thinking of Max that's driving me so crazy!*

The intercom buzzed. "One fat-free scone, please, Mary," Sarah's voice called imperiously through the speaker.

"Elizabeth," Mary ordered, not even looking up from her paperwork.

Elizabeth rinsed her hands under the tap and arranged a fresh scone—Sarah insisted they be homemade every day—on a china plate that Elizabeth knew cost more than her monthly salary.

"Be right back," she called behind her, but no one bothered to answer.

Walking through the swinging door with a heavy heart, Elizabeth knew what the problem was. The problem wasn't that she believed that nothing would ever happen between her and Max. The problem was, she was still sure that something would.

James squirmed restlessly in his carrel in Oxford University's library. This year, for some reason, he had lucked out in the lottery and received the Taj Mahal of all carrels: an extra-deep, cozy comfy corner, with a window facing into a courtyard, such that the carrel was practically like his own private little studio.

Still, it was nearing four o'clock, and he hadn't gotten anything done—fancy little study corner or not. Despite having brushed off Katrin so effectively this morning in the coffee shop, James hadn't managed to brush Vanessa off from his thoughts. He winced again at how roughly he'd put off Katrin and patted his pocket to make sure that he still had her number to pass on to his friend. *Smooth, mate. Smooth,* he berated himself.

Still, the day was waxing on, and James hadn't

accomplished anything more than buying a brioche and envisioning himself driving Vanessa through a series of winding country roads for hours while she poured them both glasses of wine and laughed frequently at his charming jokes.

James turned back a page and sighed. *Focus, James. Focus.* He was trying to sum up the effects of optimizing returns versus a simple profit-driven system of revenues, and his notes made about as much sense as if he had attempted to write them in Greek while standing on his head. He put his head down on the smooth wood of the desk and slowly exhaled. *The only revenue I want is Vanessa to let me take her out on a date,* he thought. This wasn't working.

A thought popped into his head. *Maybe it isn't working because you know you're avoiding a much bigger problem,* he cautioned himself. *Like the fact that you've fancied Vanessa for practically forever, and the most you've been able to do is stutter "hi" to the girl.* Max had actually told him just that—maybe Vanessa never acknowledged him because she was convinced he was a big, stupid wimp.

James stood and looked at the near empty library. But of *course* it was nearly empty, he told himself. Everyone else in the universe was out having a life. And he had stuck himself up in this stupid library trying to convince his parents—and himself—that he was doing something productive with his life. It was time to *have* a life also, James suddenly decided.

James shoved his endless stack of heavy, impenetrable economics books toward the back of the carrel and flipped his sheaf of articles into his briefcase. His pulse had begun to beat a little faster, and a light sweat broke out on his skin. *Just keep it calm,* he said to himself, checking his reflection in the window and making sure his little tantrum on the desk hadn't made his hair into the shape of a loaf of bread. *Just pretend that you're not going over straightaway to ask Vanessa out on a date—maybe pretend that you're going over to hang around with Max, as usual—and you won't drive off the side of the road.*

As he showed the contents of his briefcase to the scary lady at the exit who always checked for sticky-fingered students, James fumbled for some gum. Luckily he found an old stick of peppermint. Shoving it into his mouth, he restrained himself from asking the scary lady if he looked all right. *Well, Vanessa's seen the top of your head plenty of times while serving you,* he thought. *Your face is bound to be an improvement over* that.

James was again struck by the anxiety he always felt about Vanessa. "God, how am I going to overcome that maid thing?" he said to himself. It wasn't that James minded that Vanessa was a maid—far from it. The minute he'd first seen her, it hadn't mattered to him *what* job she had—she practically could have been behind bars for mass murder, and he still would have been charmed. But he suspected that Vanessa wasn't so keen on *his* job—or lack thereof. Was it that she just didn't trust his intentions? Or that she had no patience for silly Oxford boys who grew up with silver spoons in their mouths?

But that's not me! James thought wildly, fumbling for the keys to his Alfa Romeo. As he bleep-bleeped and the door flipped open, his face colored. *Well, I might be bloody rich, but it's not the* only *thing about me,* James thought. *It's as silly to hate people for being rich as it is to hate them for being poor.*

"James!" James heard a female voice call, laughing.

James turned around. Standing in the sunlight was Miriam Julian, another economics student in his year. James knew her only through departmental parties and the occasional colloquium, but he liked her well enough. "Hey, Miriam," he said, shifting his briefcase to his other hand and sliding his car keys into his pocket.

Miriam had cut her hair into a spiky bob since he'd last seen her and evidently given up her old leather minis for cargo pants and tank tops. She was actually very cute, James realized. He'd never really noticed her before—students in economics weren't the most social animals in the world.

111

"I'm glad I caught you," Miriam said, smiling shyly. "I just wanted to give you this." Sticking her hand into her knapsack, she withdrew and then held out a slim white envelope to James.

James reached out and took it from her, slightly confused. He glanced at the back, on which his name was neatly printed in ink. Was it some holiday thing? Or a joke?

"What is it?" he asked weakly, hoping that it wasn't a call for donations to some wacky cult that Miriam had just joined. Economics students were a strange lot, James knew—many of them cracked under the pressure and decided it was easier to worship the sun god Ra than seek the approval of a doctoral committee.

Miriam burst out laughing at his discomfort. "Lord, James! It's an invitation to a dinner party, that's all!" She cackled.

James blushed, he felt so silly. *This* type of behavior was probably exactly why Vanessa didn't want to go out with him—she sensed that underneath his studious, conscientious demeanor he was actually a paranoid, goofy freak.

"I'm sorry, Miriam," he said, trying to sound breezy and nonfreaky. "I'm just always worried the thesis police are around the corner or something," he added.

Miriam laughed again and moved a little closer

to him. Before James knew it, she had her hand on his arm. "Well, I'm certainly not one of them," she said, looking into James's eyes.

James almost jumped out of his skin at her touch. What kinds of pheromones was he shooting into the atmosphere today? He'd gone years—well, months, at least—without a date. Now, suddenly, seductresses were coming out of the woodwork. *I just hope Vanessa is one of them,* he thought.

His experience with Katrin had given him a dose of suavity in putting all the seductresses off, however. "Well, I'll be sure to try to make it," he said, letting her remove her hand naturally instead of jerking away like a dork.

Miriam smiled. "Do," she said. "And I'd love to read your thesis. Anytime."

Now, *that* was an offer he could take her up on. It would be neat to have Miriam as a friend anyway—he didn't have any female friends. *And I could use one now to tell me what the hell to do with Vanessa,* he thought.

Driving up toward Pennington House, James checked his teeth in the mirror repeatedly and kept the college radio station—which always blasted Sid Vicious all day long—on as loud as it would go to pump himself up. (And in his Alfa Romeo's incredibly expensive stereo system, that was pretty loud.) "I'm just going to march up and say, 'Vanessa, I'd be honored if you'd let me take you to dinner,' " he tested out. "No, that's too wimpy. 'Vanessa, may I take you to dinner?' " He frowned again, trying to decide if his teeth were too yellow and snaggly. "Too much like I'm asking her to marry me—no rushing into things. How about, 'How would you feel if I took you out sometime?' " He frowned at himself again. "Blast. Wimpy and wimpier still."

Something will come to you, he tried to tell himself as he drove up the long, winding drive.

At the door he was met by Mary, who wore a gray cardigan and an inscrutable expression, as usual. James had been picturing Vanessa answering the door, but that was unrealistic—he was actually just glad that Sarah hadn't answered. For some reason, Max's little sister had been flirting like crazy whenever she saw him lately, and James didn't think he could deal with *three* women seemingly fancying him in the same day.

"Mr. Leer," Mary said, nodding politely.

James decided the best way to make the bizarre and unprecedented—to Mary, at least—request for Vanessa's company was to make it in as no-nonsense a manner as possible. "Vanessa—," he began.

Mary arched an eyebrow, and James's mouth went completely dry. Vanessa! He'd meant to say *Mary,* of course.

James swallowed. "That is, Mary, rather. I'd like

114

to see Miss Vanessa for a moment, if that's possible."

If Mary thought anything was out of the ordinary, she gave no sign. "I believe Miss Vanessa is not in, sir," she said. "May I ask what this is regarding?"

James shot Mary a look—it wasn't like her to be so forward. Generally the only thing she inquired was if you wanted something to drink. "Don't trouble yourself, Mary," James answered, fairly sharply.

Now it was Mary's turn to color. "I only wanted to be sure it was not a matter having to do with Vanessa's duties, sir," Mary murmured, her eyes looking steely.

Now James blushed again—and felt horrible. Here he'd almost gotten Vanessa in trouble—and confused and insulted Mary as well. If this was what came of the rich running around and fraternizing with the help, he'd have to change his behavior.

"Mary, I'm so sorry," James said. "Please—it's nothing Miss Vanessa's done out of turn, I assure you." He turned around to leave, then stopped and smiled back at her. "And I thank you so much for your help today," he added.

Mary's face remained a stiff mask, but she nodded and closed the door. Well, James thought, he would be overly formal too in her position—dealing with the whims and wants of a bunch of people who didn't even toast their own bread for themselves in the morning.

Maybe I shouldn't have even opened up this whole can of worms, James thought miserably, speeding the Alfa Romeo toward his parents' house, where he was expected for dinner that evening. He thought of the cold look he'd always gotten in response to his pleading glances in Vanessa's direction. *That's certainly what Vanessa seems to think.*

But James steeled himself. *Look, if you don't go after the girl you've liked forever—if you don't just ask her out once and for all so she can turn you down—you're going to be a tortured man forever,* he decided. *And a coward too,* he added after a minute.

James thought ahead with dread to the conversation he would be greeted with at his parents' house. They would ask him how his thesis was going, then if he was seeing "anyone interesting," his parents' code words for "the girl you're going to marry."

Maybe tonight he would have the courage to tell them the truth.

Mom, Dad—I'm in love with a maid at Pennington House. And you want to know the funny part? She won't even give me the time of day.

Vanessa took a step back from the window, nearly sighing aloud with relief. James's red Alfa Romeo was speeding into the distance, with him in it. Mary must have dispatched him somehow, Vanessa thought, looking down at her hands and realizing that they were actually trembling from anxiety.

When Vanessa had chanced to see James slamming the door of his sleek red car, she had darted up the main stairway—strictly forbidden to servants, of course, but this was an *emergency*—and ducked into an empty sitting room upstairs. She wanted to make sure that Mary wouldn't send her out to bring James a series of ice waters while he pretended to wait for Max but truly just peeked around to snatch glances of her bum.

Well, that's unfair, Vanessa thought, trying to be reasonable. *James never looked at your bum—or not that you noticed. It's your eyes he always goes for, the cheeky bastard.*

Vanessa began to have a glimmer of understanding at the amount of outrage generated by James's little crush on her. As the Alfa Romeo disappeared completely around the curve in the drive, she found that she was practically clenching both her fists. *What does he think: He can buy me like he bought that car?* Vanessa seethed. *Or no,* she continued, her face forming a sneer. *I forgot—it's the Alfa Romeo his daddy bought for him, I'm sure. Perhaps he'd like to buy me from the earl—it's not like daughters aren't still sold off in plenty of countries.*

Vanessa walked over to the hall closet and yanked out the vacuum with an angry jerk. She pressed her heel firmly onto the on button and was incredibly gratified by the angry roar of reply. *Someone knows exactly how I feel*, she thought, running the heavy machine back and forth on the thick carpet. And if Mary came by and asked why she was vacuuming on a Friday (of course, vacuuming was on *Tuesday*), she'd tell her she was sucking up James's terrible "Leer."

A silly love-struck boy is the last thing I need, she thought, trying to vent her frustration by thrusting the vacuum head aggressively under the flaps of the damask-covered couch. *Some big, soft boy who'll use me up and throw me away the minute his parents say "boo,"* Vanessa thought, thinking again of her mother. Her rage grew. *He's going to pay for what he did—he's going to pay.*

What was he thinking—that she would just fall at his knees, grateful that he'd noticed her at all? His silly car could have put her through university for the last four years. It probably could have put the entire household staff through university, she decided. Didn't he have any feeling of responsibility? Didn't any of these damned people have any sense of responsibility whatsoever?

But what, exactly, had James done? Vanessa thought. He only liked her—he wasn't the one that had gotten her mother pregnant, then thrown her in the gutter.

But they're all alike, Vanessa thought furiously, not noticing that she was revacuuming the same stretch of carpet over and over again. *Taking advantage of good people who don't know any better and leaving huge messes behind for other people to clean up. That's all they do—leave a mess behind for other people to clean up.*

Vanessa was crying now, but she wasn't aware of it. *Well, I won't be stuck being the one who cleans it up this time*, she thought. *I've got my mother's mess to fix up, and I don't need a new mess to sort out.*

Finally Vanessa felt the wetness on her cheeks. She turned off the vacuum. She sat in a small chair and stared off into space.

But why do I keep thinking so angrily about James? Vanessa thought. *If he's so soft and harmless, why am I so afraid of what he's going to do?*

In her heart of hearts, Vanessa didn't think that James was like the earl at all. But hadn't the earl probably tortured her mother with those same doe eyes? Hadn't he seemed so completely, impossibly in love?

That's why I feel so worried about James, Vanessa realized. *Because he seems so—so—honest.*

She stood and wiped the tears off her cheeks. *But he's not*, she insisted to herself. *He's not. He's a big, stupid lunk and he'll use you for all you've got, just like the earl used your mother.*

Vanessa switched to the hose attachment and began to swipe the dust off the moldings. *This is all mine!* she thought. *Everything in this house is all mine, just as much as it is that brat Sarah's and that stiff Max's. But I don't even care. I just want him to pay. To pay and pay, forever.*

Vanessa shoved the vacuum back in the closet, thinking again of the photograph of her mother that she was going to steal. *But who do I want to pay for what they did?* she suddenly asked herself. *The earl? Or James?*

She plucked an incredibly large dust bunny that she'd missed off the carpet and pitched it into the trash, then stood staring into the opening of the metal can. For some reason, its empty, dark, soundless bottom seemed very significant. She had another thought.

Or do I want both of them to pay?

Max lifted his laptop from the gray stone wall and clicked it shut. Despite the fact that he was getting nowhere with his thesis—*and* his novel *and* his fiancée, his internal schoolmarm added, to his irritation—he still couldn't stop thinking about the fact that Elizabeth had asked after him earlier. *Oh, get stuffed, Max,* he told himself, trying not to get all worked up about something that would probably turn out to be nothing. *She probably just wants to ask if you can do without your regular brand of Vegemite tomorrow or something.*

Max ran his finger down the hard, graphite-colored exterior of his new laptop. It was amazing what they were doing with the things these days—this new model was as thin as some of the notebooks Max had used in primary school. Probably one day he would be able to stick his computer in his shirt pocket.

Almost as thin as the ice you're skating on right now with Lavinia too, Max thought, inwardly groaning. Well, there was that dinner tomorrow night with her aunt and uncle—that was sure to improve matters and make her feel that Max was taking the marriage as seriously as she was. *Mary certainly is,* he thought. In the past half hour he'd seen her hustling Alice and Vanessa through the dining room at least a dozen times—working out seatings and serving for the big dinner, he was sure.

Max decided he'd go inside to the house's large library, where there was less distraction—especially distraction that reminded him of his upcoming nuptials. *Maybe I'll have more luck when I'm not waiting for Elizabeth to walk by,* he admitted to himself sheepishly.

Max slipped the computer under his arm and made his way into Pennington House's large general library. Here were none of his father's famous collections—instead there were stacks of encyclopedias, bad nineteenth-century novels (Max had sampled them as a teenager, then given up in agony), and strange compilations listing wheat prices in 1943 in Sussex and other perfectly fascinating information.

Max took a seat, flipped open his laptop, and hit the icon to dial up to the Internet. As the machine whirled and clicked, Max couldn't help but smile. Just a year ago he'd had to plug his computer into the phone line in order to dial up. Now (for only thousands and thousands of pounds, he thought wryly) he was able to dial up the Internet from anywhere, all from within his computer. He smiled—being rich was good for *something*. Even if that something couldn't fix whatever problems were going between him, Lavinia, his thesis, and his novel.

His smile slowly disappeared. What was wrong with him anyway? Lavinia looked like a model; she was bright, charming, and somewhat sensitive; and still he'd spent the entire day skulking around his own house in hopes of running into the scullery maid instead of enjoying an afternoon at the theater with her. *Lavinia should be enough for me,* he thought desperately, wanting some rigid disciplinarian to stand over him with a ruler and smack him into having common sense.

But I have to be my own disciplinarian now,

Max told himself. *And I'm doing a decidedly un-brilliant job of it too.*

He looked at the screen in front of him, glowing a soft green. On the left side, neatly lined up, were the trash, his novel icon, and his thesis icon.

Max gave a little bark of laughter—it was too perfect. Which one was going to be allowed to be completed? Which one was going to go in the trash?

He was beginning to irritate himself. *If I try to write this novel, I'm shirking my responsibilities,* he thought. *But if I do the thesis and marry Lavinia, I'm ignoring everything that makes me me. How did Father accept all of these responsibilities that had nothing to do with him without losing himself in the process?*

Max double clicked on his novel icon, and the screen suddenly expanded into his scattered notes—only about twenty pages' worth, all told. He was filled with disgust for himself. *Novel,* he thought. *More like a pamphlet.*

He turned away from the screen, looking at a row of unread books. *If I try to write this book, everyone's going to think I'm some horrid dilettante—like Prince Charles and his bloody watercolors.* A vision came into his head of him burrowing away in his study, an aged, white-haired madman, while Lavinia and his children shook their heads in dismay.

Prince Charles. Diana. Charles and Camilla. *Now, there's a man who married the woman he was supposed to marry and never forgot the woman he loved,* Max thought.

That's my problem, Max abruptly realized. *I muck about, but I never really do one thing or the other. I could be a writer, or I could be like Dad and be in Parliament, but if I never decide, I'm just going to be a man who only knows how to feel sorry for himself. And if I'm always going to be such a stupid, indecisive guy, I might as well chuck it all now and marry Lavinia. Or anyone. Because whoever I am, I'm not going to be worth much of anything.*

Suddenly inspired, Max found a search engine and plugged in the words *Sweet Valley University.* Right away he was taken to the site. His breathing became a little faster. He put in the words *Elizabeth Bennet.*

Immediately the search path put him off. *No results were found* blinked up.

Max tried again, spelling *Bennet* differently. Again the search was unsuccessful.

Max leaned back. Maybe they only listed students who were currently enrolled. That must be it.

Otherwise, Max thought, Max Pennington wasn't the only one with something to hide.

Chapter
Six

Elizabeth knocked gently on Sarah's door, deftly balancing the scone on its china plate in one hand. There was no answer, and she leaned in closer. "But I won't even know half the blokes there!" she heard Sarah's high voice chirrup, then she burst out laughing. "No, no—you're right, Vic. You're totally right."

Sarah must be talking on the phone, Elizabeth thought. She leaned back, then knocked a little louder. "Sarah?" she asked. No response.

Suddenly Elizabeth flashed back to the numerous times she had pounded on Jessica's door at their old house in Sweet Valley, screaming over the stereo for Jessica to come help with dinner or do the laundry. And how often had Jessica simply answered and flounced out to the beach or a date, leaving Elizabeth to do all the work at home?

Well, I'm sure banging on Sarah's door wildly would be considered "improper" in my particular position, Elizabeth thought, wondering how to manage her scone delivery efficiently and politely. Nonetheless, Elizabeth wasn't able to completely conceal her impatience with Pennington's princess. She knocked as loudly as she felt she safely could. "Sarah!" she called, raising her voice.

Suddenly the door was wrenched open from the inside. Sarah stood, in a slip and tights, her phone in one hand, looking at Elizabeth blankly. "Put it over there," Sarah finally ordered, jerking her head toward the night table.

Elizabeth restrained the urge to pop the scone in her own mouth and chew it while smiling widely at the spoiled little snot. *I knew something was up,* she thought, imagining that she was Anthony Hopkins in *The Remains of the Day* in order to maintain her composure. *Or why would Sarah be so lovey-dovey with me in the dining room and so awful when nobody else is around?*

"But I don't like the way the blue shirt makes my skin look green," Sarah was moaning. "Also, I've got four new spots."

Elizabeth smiled to herself as she placed the scone carefully on the night table. Sarah Pennington didn't have a single pimple on her perfect complexion. It was reassuring to know that girls still gossiped constantly about what made them look how and whether or not it was true that the New York skyline was rising up on their foreheads. *The more things change,* she thought, noting how she still wasn't above checking herself in the mirror when a certain Mr. Pennington was around.

Sarah was standing in front of her mirror, nodding emphatically as she listened to whoever was excitedly chattering on the other line. "Uh-huh," Sarah said, fingering a long, blue dress. "Of course he will, you idiot. But what am I supposed to say back to him?"

Elizabeth stopped in her tracks, her conversation with the earl suddenly seeming incredibly relevant. *Sarah is talking about a boy, of course,* Elizabeth thought. *Does that mean I jump on her with leg irons right now?*

Or maybe she should just wait outside, then reenter and tell Sarah all the facts about men dating and relationships—*Like how your sister will destroy your entire life when she fools around with your ex,* Elizabeth found herself thinking. Whoa—if she talked to Sarah in this state of mind, she'd come off like some boozy divorcée. *Also,* Elizabeth decided, *if I talk to her now, she'll just think I've been eavesdropping—which, frankly, I have. That's exactly the way to* not *win over a sixteen-year-old.*

Elizabeth opened the door and was about to

duck silently into the hall when Sarah's voice rose after her. "Um, Elizabeth," Sarah called.

Elizabeth put her head back in through the doorway. "Yes, Sarah?" she asked, inwardly begging that Sarah wasn't about to accuse her of listening in—or having delivered a stale scone.

But Sarah gave her an innocent smile. "Max was looking for you earlier," she said simply, putting the receiver back to her ear to forestall any further conversation.

Elizabeth flushed all over, the statement reacting to her system like a heat-seeking missile. Max had been looking for her? Why? What for? *I don't care,* Elizabeth thought. The fact that he was seeking—had sought—her out was enough of a thrill to keep her going for the rest of the day—the rest of her stay in London, if necessary.

Elizabeth fought the urge to ask Sarah why Max was looking for her, then found herself unable to resist it. "Excuse me, Sarah," Elizabeth said, ducking her head back in quickly and wincing at her execrable syntax, "but do you know what Max was looking for me for?"

Sarah only shrugged, her cherubic face unreadable. "Max didn't say," she said. But when Elizabeth turned again to go, she stopped her again. "Oh, and Elizabeth? If anyone asks where I am, I'm popping over to . . .Victoria's to study,"

128

Sarah finished, her eyes flitting away from Elizabeth's to the mirror oddly.

Elizabeth had an almost visceral sense that Sarah was lying—her voice had had that planned nonchalance teenagers depended on that never quite rang true. But at the same time, if Sarah really was running out to meet a guy, Elizabeth felt that there was very little she could do about it. For instance, what would an appropriate action be? To run down to the earl and tell him that his daughter might be about to meet with "a boy"? To find Max and ask him if his sister ever truly studied at Victoria's? *Enough*, Elizabeth thought. *I already decided I wasn't going to turn Sarah in to the Pennington police. I'll talk to her later—after I talk to Max,* she was unable to help adding.

"All right," Elizabeth said, walking back into the hall. Immediately she heard Sarah's intense conversation resume. "But don't you think the plaid is so juvenile?" Sarah's voice asked, sounding like she was worried some global treaty might collapse if it were so.

Elizabeth felt a sudden rush of longing for her old friend Nina Harper—for Nina's old, comfortable room, her warm eyes, and her sage advice, most particularly. *I'll probably never speak to Nina again,* Elizabeth thought miserably.

But another thought pricked its way to the

surface. *Why shouldn't I speak to Nina again?* Elizabeth asked herself. *Or even just e-mail her? It's not like I'm in another space-time continuum. I'm just in London.*

Well, first of all, you don't have e-mail, Elizabeth answered herself. *And it's not like you can really march up to Max or Sarah and ask to get onto their e-mail accounts.*

But maybe you could, Elizabeth thought, continuing the internal argument. *I'm sure Max would let you—happily.*

But Elizabeth's stomach twisted oddly at that suggestion. *No, it's too weird,* she thought. *I'd like to think we're friends, but the fact of the matter is, I serve him his breakfast in the morning—and I don't want him giving me charity, which is how he'd see it. Not like that's not totally your fault.*

Another problem occurred to her, and Elizabeth stopped dead in her tracks. *I mean, what if he just said no?* she thought. *Max seems like such a friendly guy and everything, but I keep getting stopped dead in my tracks by the earl, don't I? Maybe this is one of those situations in which Max might gently have to school you in the realities of employer-employee relations.*

She had a sudden image of a lecture from Mary—or even some humiliating public spectacle wherein the earl walked in on both of them. *Too weird, too dangerous, no way,* Elizabeth decided, shaking her head.

She opened the doorway to the narrow back stairwell that led down to the kitchen and slowly began to creep down. *I mean, can't you see the difference between this staircase and the one that the family uses?* Her knees bumped against the white-washed walls as she pictured the marble expanse at the front of Pennington House. *Get to know your place, Elizabeth.*

There was another problem. *Nina might tell your parents where you are,* Elizabeth realized. *And right now, you have enough problems without your family assaulting you from overseas—or from some hotel room in the city.*

Elizabeth let her fingers trace the walls lightly and stood for a second, listening to the bustle from below and the silence from above. She was fighting off the memory of a party at the end of her sophomore year in college, just before she'd gone off on the road trip with Sam and Jessica over the summer. Nina had been there, looking beautiful, and she, Nina, and Jessica had danced wildly, so excited about the future that it seemed they could taste it. *Who knew it would taste like this?* Elizabeth thought, smelling the damp of the dark stairway.

She tried to stifle the lump that was rising in

her throat. Pulling a spare rag out of her pocket, she dabbed at her eyes, clearing her throat so that she wouldn't sound husky when answering one of Cook or Mary's demands—several must have built up in the time she'd been away delivering the scone. *I knew that growing up would involve a lot of difficult changes,* Elizabeth thought, slowly beginning the long walk down, incredulous that she really was too scared to e-mail her best friend. *I just didn't know that one of the changes would leave me completely alone.*

"All right, Vic. Gotta motor," Sarah said, glancing at the clock. One part of her was happier gossiping about the meeting with Nick than actually meeting him, but she knew she had to actually go at some point—she'd soon have nothing more to gossip about if she simply stayed home.

"Call me *immediately* afterward and tell me *everything,*" Victoria hissed, talking as if she were passing on the code for a neutron bomb. "Don't you dare go to bed without phoning!"

"All right," Sarah said, secretly thrilled that she was the one in possession of all the attention and not the other way round. *God, could you imagine if I had to listen to Victoria jaw on and on about some bloke?* she thought, practically shuddering at the thought. *Thank God Nick fancied me and not Vic.*

"All right, darling. Talk to you soon. Cheers," Sarah said, imitating Lavinia's icy efficiency. As she hung up, she could still hear Victoria's nervous sputters over the line: "Don't forget! Don't forget to call!"

Sarah turned to her wardrobe, shaking her head. As usual, she wasn't able to decide on anything that she felt sufficiently flattered her for the evening—especially since she was going to be meeting all sorts of strangers as well. She fingered a long, red jersey dress. No. Too fancy—and perhaps too come-hither as well. *I'm having enough trouble thinking about tomorrow night already without encouraging Nick,* Sarah thought. She looked at the jeans and cardigan she always wore on weekends, currently crumpled in a heap in the center of the carpet. Ugh. She wanted Nick to respect her for more than her looks, but she wasn't trying to send the message that she didn't care about how she looked at all. *Anyway, Nick likes it when I dress up,* she thought, getting slightly gooey at the memory of how, when they'd first met, he'd always complimented her on her clothing and how well she wore it.

Sarah considered a lovely pair of black silk pants that she'd bought with Victoria last summer at some street sale but then decided that those were really *too* wild. Anyway, she had always envisioned herself wearing them at a party and enticing Wills with them—knocking Britney Spears and whoever else he fancied out of the running. She smiled at the fantasy, Wills pushing them aside while he made a beeline for her across a crowded room.

The only man who's going to ask, "Who's the girl in the pants?" Sarah thought with some satisfaction, *is the future king of England.*

Her eyes fell on an outfit she'd bought last year but never worn: a black wool pleated miniskirt and a V-necked cashmere sweater, both bought on a jaunt to Paris after Christmas with the earl. They had escaped notice because the fabrics felt too fine for school, while the style was too casual for most events. *But they're perfect for tonight,* Sarah thought, her eyes lighting up as she seized the garments and threw them on, stopping to examine herself in the mirror.

Why, I look at least seventeen! Sarah exclaimed inwardly, amazed at how the skirt lengthened her legs while the sweater gave her the barest hint of adult cleavage. *Sexy but not slutty,* she decided. *Nick's going to melt.*

Giving her hair one last whack with her brush, Sarah artfully arranged her bangs to cover the four or five zits she'd decided she'd developed since that morning, pinching her cheeks to put some blood in them. *The Guinness will give me some color, if nothing else,* Sarah thought, giggling, remembering that her tryst with Nick was going to take place at a pub.

Sporting her satchel defensively over her front like some medieval knight's shield, Sarah darted out of her room and out the door, silently thanking the fates that she hadn't run into her father or Max on the way out—which would have involved a bit of fast talking she was loath to engage in, preferring to concentrate on Nick's last kiss that morning. She felt the tingle on her neck where he'd kissed her and touched the spot, sighing. What was her name again?

Fenwick was outside, fiddling with the limo, as usual. Sarah heaved another sigh of relief—tracking him down would have involved telling Mary as well as Elizabeth her destination, and Mary was much more likely to have a conversation with the earl before Sarah was back. "I'm going to Victoria's, Fenwick," she clipped sharply, silently urging him to pop to attention as quickly as possible.

Luckily Fenwick complied. "Yes, miss," he said, his face betraying no hint of worry or hesitation. Good. That meant the earl hadn't declared that she must vet all travel through him. *I've got this one chance to have a life,* Sarah thought, *and I'm going to use it.*

Settling in the back of the limo, Sarah's nervousness about being caught by her father became spine-tingling anticipation about her date with

Nick. Ignoring Fenwick as much as possible, Sarah flipped down the lighted passenger's mirror on the back of the front seats and pulled out her favorite lipstick—a deep plum she'd bought recently on a school trip to Prague.

Trying to overcome the occasional jounce in the road, Sarah carefully lined her mouth, then blotted on the back of a school assignment she found crumpled into her purse. She looked at herself with pleasure. The lipstick somehow brought her entire face together, making its planes sharper, more dramatic. *I look like a French exchange student named Geneviève,* Sarah thought, delighted. *Not an ordinary English girl.*

Sarah flipped the mirror shut and leaned back, wanting to shout with joy that she'd escaped the house so easily and at the prospect of an entire evening—like grown-ups!—spent with Nick. *I just want to run into the woods and dance around with glee,* Sarah thought, stretching her legs out in front of her in giddy excitement.

Suddenly a somewhat deflating realization struck her. *Is this how Daddy used to make Mummy feel?* she thought, wondering whether that made her feel happy, sad, or queer.

Queer, Sarah finally decided. *Definitely, definitely queer.*

*   *   *

Vanessa had just finished steaming the velvety carpet in one of the upstairs bedrooms when Mary's squawk sounded over the general intercom. "Mary, Alice, and Elizabeth, report to the office immediately, please," she said.

Vanessa turned off the steamer with an impatient jerk. "Office"—ha! As if a little table crowded behind nine thousand kitchen implements equaled an office.

Returning the steamer to the utility closet, Vanessa wondered vaguely what Mary could be on about. Were they going to have to go over the plans for the dinner tomorrow yet *again*? Vanessa had seen Mary dragging Alice all over the dining room earlier and fled upstairs in response. "You'd think the queen herself was coming here for tea," Vanessa muttered, suddenly realizing that Lavinia, as a duchess, wasn't so far from the throne herself. *Yes, but neither am I, if you look at it like that,* Vanessa thought. *When I serve them, it'll be the prince-and-the-pauper mix-up all over again.*

Grumpily entering the kitchen, Vanessa gave a perfunctory nod to both Elizabeth and Alice, who both looked like they'd been dragged through the coal bin. Taking a seat across from the stone-faced Mary, Vanessa looked at her own grubby hands, then hid them quickly in her lap. *Guess I'm not so shining clean myself,* she thought, noticing that all three of them shared the same pink eyes and noses that came from an undue exposure to dust and chemical solvents.

"I've called you all here today because we have a large project that concerns the household staff primarily," Mary said primly, adjusting her half-moon glasses so that she could give them each a baleful glance. Vanessa noted with scorn that Mary had stacked in front of her a large sheaf of papers, like they were about to argue a case in front of a judge or something. *I'd like to argue that we lock up the earl and throw away the key,* Vanessa thought, jiggling her knee with impatience. *And we could donate this whole house to charity and make it a haven for parents who don't want their children.*

"You all know that tomorrow we are to entertain Sir Pennington, Junior's, fiancée, Miss Lavinia," Mary continued, adopting the slightly high-flown accent she used whenever discussing the royal members of the household. Vanessa detested her for it. *What do we need all of these bloody meetings for?* Vanessa thought. *Next thing you know, we'll have to take a vote to see if we'll be putting salted butter or sweet with the rolls.*

"What you also know," Mary went on, the accent rising up into a high tremolo—like she was a batty old lady talking about her beautiful youth on an omnibus, Vanessa thought—"is that the wedding is to be held here, on the grounds of Pennington House at . . . Christmas!"

Mary paused for effect, bestowing on all three girls a beneficent smile that let them know just how lucky they all were to be party to—and partly involved in—this information. All three girls had decidedly undecided reactions, however. Vanessa's stomach immediately contracted in dismay and outrage—as if she even wanted to think about having that stupid wedding here in the middle of the holiday season. All that could mean was a bloody lot of extra work for which they wouldn't be paid, thank you very much. Elizabeth's face looked merely wooden—*She's probably wishing she hadn't let her crush on Max run so far,* Vanessa thought with more joy than she should have had. And Alice—poor, dipsy Alice—merely echoed Mary's satisfied pronouncement with a vaguely enthusiastic titter, then lapsed into a state of nervous suspension.

"Will the wedding be catered?" Vanessa asked suddenly. She had been thinking with irritation of all the extra duties that entertaining guests in the house would entail—working on call until late into the night to bring bourbon and soda to chattering masses, fluffing up twelve bedrooms a morning instead of three—when she suddenly realized that the horrors could be increased exponentially if they were expected to completely feed and fetch for hundreds of people as well. *But there's only three of us, and Lavinia's sure to want an enormous wedding!* Vanessa thought, trying to calm herself. *There's no way we'll be expected to manage the events and the cake as well.*

"The cake will come from Menninger's," Mary intoned, naming the most exclusive patisserie in all of London as if she were reading Vanessa's mind. "But the rest of the wedding will be catered exclusively by Pennington House."

This announcement did yield a general cry of dismay. "But how can we possibly—," Alice broke out, just as Elizabeth's incredulous, "Really?" got tangled with Vanessa's, "You can't be serious!"

"Girls, girls," Mary said, holding up her hands in an exaggerated gesture of impatience. "Please, now."

Why, the old bat is enjoying every minute of this! Vanessa realized, her rage doubling. *She's just been waiting for some huge event like this, where she can play the great leader and we'll all be forced to play the lowly slaves!*

Uncharacteristically, Elizabeth offered a dissenting opinion, her voice quiet and measured. "It does seem like quite a lot of work for such a small staff," she offered, giving Mary a timid smile.

Mary did not return it. "It seems unwise to comment on the amount of work one may have to do or must do before one is aware of what the amount of work *is*," Mary said, giving Elizabeth a withering look. Vanessa wanted to hoot at Mary's tangled imitation of high-class grammar, but she was too perturbed by this new information. Elizabeth shrank under Mary's fierce stare. "In any case, we will of course take on additional staff as needed," Mary added, fixing her steely glare on all of them.

Yeah, like some dopey bloke with spots to mop up after we've cleared away the nine thousand plates, Vanessa thought in agony. *I know I wanted to punish my father, but really—is it worth all this?*

Mary began to give them a speech about how they would be representing all that Pennington House—and England—stood for (dignity and civility) evidently, then began to read off a long list of the preliminary guests to be expected at the wedding. "Lucrezia Thalbert-Quackenbush and Lord Nodoff-Hughley-Dooley the Ninth," Alice whispered across to Vanessa after the incredibly large series of preposterous names came to an end.

Mary glared at Alice. "This type of insolence won't be tolerated," she said sharply. "You will not only be representing Pennington House at this wedding, but the earl and myself," she said, as if they were going to be married. "If you do not feel you are capable of fulfilling your duties in an acceptable manner, please say so now."

Alice fairly collapsed under Mary's admonition. Vanessa had to restrain the urge to get up and comfort her and shake her finger in Mary's face. *Why, Mary knows that Alice depends on this job to look after her mum in Shropshire,* she thought. *She's got no right to torture Alice just because Miss Lavinia Idiotica can't even plan her own stupid wedding.*

Instead Vanessa merely asked another question to which she didn't want to hear the answer. "I suppose this will all take place over a weekend?" she asked.

Mary flushed with pleasure. "That's correct. However, we've got lots of time, since it's only September and the wedding isn't until late December," she said, clasping her hands as if it were her own son who was to be married. *Well, I'm sure it feels like that to her,* Vanessa thought, inwardly shaking her head at the delusions some people needed. *One thing you'll never catch me doing,* Vanessa added to herself, *is confusing the people whose toilets I clean with my family.*

She jerked noticeably. *Of course, in my case, they really are the same thing,* Vanessa realized, her hands curling into fists under the table.

"Does that conflict with any plans of yours, Vanessa?" Mary asked sarcastically.

Only my plan to shove your face in a big bowl of

oyster stew, Vanessa thought nastily. But she wasn't her mother's daughter for nothing—she knew what could come of losing control of your emotions. "Oh, no," Vanessa said politely, giving Mary a tidy smile.

"Good," Mary said, and proceeded to divvy duties and wings up between the three girls, passing around small note cards that specified certain areas in clear blue ink. "We will, of course, serve high tea on Saturday," Mary continued, her voice rising and falling as if she were singing an aria to her assembled fans.

Vanessa looked at her two fellow maids. For the first time she felt a distinct kinship with them. As they examined the cards and listened to Mary's endless stream of tasks and duties, Vanessa was sure they were all thinking exactly the same thing:

We don't get paid nearly enough for this rot.

Chapter
Seven

Having added a two-hundred-word paragraph to the introduction of his thesis (that is, counting various chapter headings and additions of new explanatory *which* clauses), Max decided it was time to take a break. *Oh, don't even fool yourself, mate,* he said to himself in disgust as he folded his computer in half and tucked it under his arm. *You know you're just going to have a peek to see if Elizabeth Bennet—or whatever her name is—is anywhere about.*

Max spied her almost immediately, sitting exactly where he'd hoped she'd be—on the stone wall that she always favored in the late afternoon. As usual, she was beavering away like mad at her journal, making Max feel even more like a failure than he'd felt that morning. *Max, this girl works as a maid all day, and she still finds time and disci-*

pline enough to write, he berated himself. *You have nothing else to do, and consequently you get nothing done.*

Perhaps I should take a position as a butler somewhere and see if that works, Max joked to himself, momentarily wondering if that actually would make a difference. *Nope. No matter. Even if I lost all my money, I'd still feel that I'd been so incredibly advantaged my entire life, I'd have no business doing anything that didn't improve the lot of the common man immeasurably.*

Striding toward Elizabeth, Max tried to think of how to make his visit with her seem friendly and unplanned—*as opposed to stalkerlike and presumptuous,* he thought, grimacing. *I'll ask her a computer question,* he decided. *Something I actually need to know. After all, she is the only one in the house who'd have the faintest chance of being able to help me.*

And then I'll ask her why she was looking for me, he added, still experiencing that momentary shiver of anticipation.

Delighted with his clever ruse, Max felt free enough to plant a large smile on his face. "Elizabeth," he called, marching over and installing himself directly in her line of vision. "I apologize for disturbing you, but I wonder if I could trouble you with a quick question."

Lord, she's pretty, Max thought as Elizabeth jerked out of her journal as if from a dream. *But just because you can't get any writing done doesn't mean you have the right to interrupt other writers,* Max's practical side informed him impatiently. *Even if the person in question is unquestionably gorgeous?* Max shot back, staring into Elizabeth's clear blue-green eyes.

But Elizabeth didn't look at all troubled by the request. She smiled—beautifully, Max thought—and gestured to the space beside her. "Ask me anything you want," she joked. "As long as you're aware that I probably don't know the answer."

Modest too, Max thought with wonder, aware of how imperious Lavinia could become when interrupted, as if the catalog she was skimming was of the utmost importance. *Let Lavinia alone,* Max's practical side broke in again. *She's the woman you're going to marry—you've got to leave off comparing her to other women all the time.*

"It's just a little problem I'm having with my word-processing program," Max said, all the while thinking, *But I don't compare her to other women— just to Elizabeth.* "I can't seem to figure out the footnote function," he said, opening the sleek notebook and setting it on both his and Elizabeth's knees.

An immediate current of—*something*—passed

between them. Had Elizabeth felt it? Max was too afraid to look and see if Elizabeth was blushing like he was.

"Wow!" Elizabeth exclaimed, turning around the notebook with her fingers. She gave Max a delighted grin. "Your computer looks like it could power the space shuttle!" she said enthusiastically.

Max smiled. "Luckily that won't be necessary," he said, trying to be witty. And—luckily—Elizabeth burst out laughing.

"Well," she said, after composing herself, "this is just the same as the computer I used at home." She double clicked on the writing icon, and the program opened up. Immediately she went through a dizzying sequence, opening parts of the menu Max had never even noticed before.

"Wait, do that again for me, will you?" he asked, peering closer into the screen. Their elbows brushed, and Elizabeth jumped back. "Oh, sorry!" they both said simultaneously.

Max's face flushed, and he tried to hide his discomfort. *Look, mate, she's sorry for you, and she's being nice,* he told himself. *Don't press your luck.*

But Elizabeth's soft voice was nearly driving him crazy. "Then you go into 'insert,'" she was saying, wielding the smooth mouse with enviable alacrity. "And this field opens up—see?"

Max nodded, trying not to let the scent of

flowers overwhelm him. *Listen, you're in the garden with a beautiful girl,* he told himself. *It's natural that you would want to smother her in kisses.*

But then why didn't he ever want to kiss Lavinia when they were in romantic situations, as they had been a thousand times?

By now Elizabeth had guided him through the process a couple of times. "This must be why you were looking for me," she said, fooling around with some of the other programs he had never noticed. "Sarah said you were looking for me," she added, when he turned to her in surprise. "It *is* true that Americans are practically raised in front of computers." She laughed.

Had Elizabeth just misspoken? Or had Sarah? "But Sarah told me that you were looking for me," he said gently, the bottom falling ever so slightly out of his bubble of happiness.

Elizabeth shook her head very slowly. "No, I wasn't," she said quietly.

Well, at least she didn't say, "What would I be looking for you for, you dotty bloke?" Max thought unhappily. Had Sarah merely misunderstood something? Or was she scheming and running around, as usual? He'd have to have a talk with her and figure things out.

But not with Elizabeth. "Must be some error," he said. "But I'm very glad to have the chance to talk with you, all the same."

A smile replaced the worried look on Elizabeth's face. "Oh, I always enjoy our talks," she said.

Well, what do you expect her to say? She does work for your family, after all, Max thought. Still, he so wanted to believe that Elizabeth's smile—and enjoyment—were all real and unfeigned.

And all for him, Max thought.

Max moved a little closer to Elizabeth without thinking about it. He couldn't help himself. Talking to Elizabeth made him feel a combination of things—how he'd felt at Oxford, sitting around someone's common room and reciting the pretentious poems in the literary magazine with exaggerated accents; how he'd felt in second grade whenever he'd stumbled near Camille, a raven-haired Iraqi beauty who had remained utterly immune to his charms. It even brought back early memories of the comfort he'd felt with his father and mother in the old flat they used to keep in London, while his father was still a barrister, before his mother had died and his father had entered Parliament.

When he was with Lavinia, he felt nothing but anxiety and a vague boredom.

Stop it, Max, he told himself. *Don't ruin these nice talks with Elizabeth with thoughts of your plague of a marriage.*

However, Elizabeth's next statement made that impossible. "So, your fiancée is coming to dinner tomorrow," she said with a bright smile.

Max's hopes fell. Elizabeth couldn't have any feelings for him if she was running around chatting about his fiancée—could she?

"Oh, yes—you know, these formal dinners," he said, trying to indicate that it was no big deal. He could feel the tips of his ears get red. *Lavinia would throw a blue fit if she heard me talking about the great matrimonial feast this way,* he thought.

Elizabeth seemed to feel the same way. "Don't let Mary hear that!" she said. "Vanessa and I are worried she's going to put us into your father's tuxedos for the event." She blanched and covered her mouth. "Don't tell me I said that aloud!"

Max laughed. "I'm sure you'd look very fetching indeed," he said, leaning over her journal. "Would you mind if I asked what you're working on today?"

Elizabeth blushed and shook her head quickly. "Oh, you don't want to read this old thing," she said, closing the journal and pushing it farther away from Max's reach.

"Don't worry—I understand the sanctity of a writer's first draft. I just really am interested," Max said, and realized that he was. He wanted to know everything about this strange girl: where she was from, what type of writing she did, what books she liked. That seemed so normal and natural, unlike the forced way he always felt with Lavinia. But what was he supposed to do? What was proper, or what felt natural?

A crinkle appeared on Elizabeth's forehead as she thought about how to respond, and Max thought how desperately cute she was. He had to restrain himself from reaching out and touching the tip of her nose—luckily Elizabeth started to discourse on the differences between journalism and fiction.

"I used to think that my journalism was an effort to get at the absolute truth of things," she said, staring intently at the one open window in the house, where the shutter was banging back and forth. "But sometimes fiction strikes me as a deeper kind of truth. . . ."

As she spoke, Max took pleasure in both the lovely curve of her jaw and her words. She was so bright, so lively, so—open to life, he decided. That prompted another thought.

Did he want to *be* with Elizabeth, or did he just want to be *like* her?

"I know exactly what you mean," Max said, thinking that he sounded like he was lying, even though he knew exactly what Elizabeth was talking about.

Elizabeth turned to him. "You do?" she said.

*   *   *

As they had planned, Sarah met Nick behind the rosebushes at school—where she'd had Fenwick drop her off, claiming that she had to pick up some books she'd forgotten before she headed over to Victoria's. Nick was wearing the same jeans, T-shirt, and loose jacket he'd been wearing that day in school, but somehow he appeared transformed: Tall, graceful, and prepossessing, he looked like every archetype of "boyfriend" that had ever graced the insides of a magazine.

"Saints alive, you look fantastic," Nick whispered, his eyes twinkling as he leaned in for a kiss. Sarah raised herself onto her toes to meet him, then withdrew as she snagged her sleeve on a thorn. "Damn," she said, trying to disentangle herself from the rosebush without destroying the finely woven fabric.

Nick reached down, plucked the arm off as easy as you please, then kissed Sarah before she could thank him. "Let's head to the pub, shall we?" he asked, holding his arm out to clear a path for her through the branches.

You always make everything all right, Nick, she wanted to say, but that sounded so sappy. She didn't want him to think that she was about to demand a ring or that she was helpless without him, after all. But she couldn't very well say, *It's ripping fun to have this great big strong boyfriend to go about with!* to him either, could she?

The pub Nick had chosen was actually very close to the school, to Sarah's surprise, near where Nick had grown up. "Me mates and I still like to meet up 'ere sometimes," Nick said, his accent suddenly becoming far more strong and rough. Sarah looked up at him in surprise, but Nick merely held open the door and gestured for her to step in.

The place looked like it had been liberally washed with beer, then trampled by a herd of muddy, pissed-off elephants, Sarah decided. From the outside it had been completely nondescript, but inside it was dank, close, dirty, and dark, with a smell closer to that of a latrine than a place that served fish-and-chips on a regular basis.

Get me out of here, Sarah wanted to scream, actually freezing in her tracks. But Nick didn't notice. "Let's take that corner table," he said, leading Sarah over to the dirtiest, ricketiest, loudest seat in the place.

"All right," Sarah murmured, unable to do anything but cling closely to Nick's side. She felt, absurdly, that if he so much as left her to get a pint at the bar, she might faint. When Nick had said "local pub," she had pictured your normal London drinkery: crumbling moldings, a dark wood bar, some Scottish bartender explaining which kick had won which game while pointing at all the pictures of rugby players on the wall.

But this was some . . . *forgotten corner of hell,* Sarah decided. "Has it changed much since you were a child?" she heard herself asking Nick faintly.

Nick grinned and slapped the table. " 'At's the wunnerful thing!" he said enthusiastically. "She ain't changed a bit, not one bit, in all these years."

Maybe it's some bloke thing that I don't understand, Sarah thought, trying to relax. So it wasn't the picturesque bar she had imagined—so what? They could still have a good time. *Like how men want to return to the primordial ooze—the* actual *primordial ooze,* she thought, looking in despair at the fine toes of her leather shoes touching the filthy, wet floor.

But did that mean Nick also had to forget everything he'd learned at school—even how to speak English properly?

Responding to some secret signal of Nick's that Sarah hadn't even noticed, the bartender plopped two huge pints of black, frothy Guinness in front of them. "Oh, I couldn't," Sarah murmured, hating how she sounded like such a priss. She never drank, though, not after the time she had consumed eight Tom Collinses at her cousin's wedding and chucked them all behind the largest floral arrangement.

Sarah had *planned* with Victoria what she

would do when Nick asked her if she wanted a drink. She was going to say, "No, thanks—I don't want to feel sick *tomorrow*," looking at Nick suggestively. But with the actual pint on the table, that felt silly—what kind of person felt like one beer would affect anything?

Anyway, she didn't want to do anything to encourage Nick about tomorrow—especially when she still wasn't ready to think about what might happen when they were alone in his mother's house, without a Fenwick or an earl anywhere in sight.

"So, luv," Nick brayed, raising his pint glass high and lifting his eyebrows for her to do the same, "isn't this place great?"

For a minute Sarah was convinced that Nick was joking—this whole thing had just been a trick to poke fun at Sarah's titled world, and it would all cease in a moment, they would go to a regular pub, and she would feel like she knew the boy across from her again.

But the moment didn't come. Nick didn't break into giggles, put down his glass, or offer to take Sarah off someplace where she wouldn't be afraid to use the lavatory.

Nick put down his glass with a bang when Sarah didn't raise hers to touch his. "Oh," he said finally, a sour look coming onto his face.

Sarah leaned forward hurriedly to take a sip

from her beer. Perhaps if she forced herself just a little, she could convince Nick that she really liked the place. She'd convinced her family of all sorts of things that weren't true, hadn't she?

But I don't want to have to lie to Nick, Sarah thought miserably. *Nick's the person I don't have to lie to.*

Nick's eyes were burning. "You don't like the place, do you?" he said, his voice sounding rougher and more angry than she'd ever heard it. His face twisted with scorn, and Sarah felt like she was looking at a stranger. "It's not posh enough for a princess like you, is that it?" he asked.

Sarah felt the one sip she'd taken of the beer go down like fire. "Nick," she gasped. "Let's not do this."

But Nick was spinning out of control, and Sarah had absolutely no idea how to calm him down. He wasn't anything like her father, who could be bought off easily with a few lies—Nick had principles.

Nick took a huge gulp of beer and tapped the table, grinning widely—a huge, sneering, terrible grin, Sarah thought. "Well, miss, look about you and get stuck in because this is the *real* England," he rasped. "And if you can't take it, you can go and get stuffed because that's what all you royals will have to do any day now anyway," Nick finished, lifting and draining the pint in a series of long swallows. Sarah watched in amazement. Who was this awful man, first of all, and how had he managed to finish that pint in a matter of minutes?

"Nick, please stop it," Sarah said, trying to sound firm. "You're being silly—you know you are."

Nick shook his head, looking at Sarah like she was a bit of dirt clinging to the sole of his shoe. "You just don't get it, do you?" he asked.

Sarah leaned across the table, searching for any hint of the Nick who'd kissed her and spoken so kindly to her just hours ago in the empty classroom. "Nick, I think you're sick," Sarah finally burst out desperately, hoping she could get him out of the bar before anything truly disturbing happened.

Nick actually pointed at Sarah. "It's you who's sick," he said, his tone changing to a menacing, deathly quiet.

Sarah swallowed and opened her mouth, but Nick wasn't done. "I've seen it ever since we've been going out," he began, leaning over to take a sip from her almost untouched beer. "You don't know anything about the real world. You put on airs and go about with your fancy friends and your fancy cell phones, but you might as well be dragged to school in a rickshaw for all that you have a sense of the real world."

Sarah had a sudden vision of Fenwick dragging a rickshaw and had to choke down a sudden laugh. Fenwick was too skinny to pull a rickshaw even if it was empty anyway.

"Nick," she said, smiling at him with what she hoped was the full wattage of her beauty. He'd be swayed by her beauty if nothing else, wouldn't he? "Let's stop all this silliness and go, shall we? I know a fun place—"

But Nick wouldn't be persuaded. "*This* is a place," he insisted. "It's the type of place girls like you never see, and now you've seen it. I should have known you'd react like this. It's pathetic, really." Nick shook his head and drained half of her beer. He leaned in closer to her, and Sarah wanted to jump away from his fervent, intense gaze. "Do you see that man over there? And there? They can't get jobs. They're on the dole. Because of the laws men like your father pass in Parliament." And Nick leaned back as if he'd like to blast Parliament—and Sarah—away with his next breath.

Men like my father are responsible for that fat lout over there? Sarah thought, looking at a rancid old specimen who was barely contained by his ragged jeans and wanting to laugh. What in the world was Nick talking about?

"And why do you think these men are in the bars at five o'clock in the evening?" Nick said, looking at his nonexistent watch. His voice had dropped to a low hiss. "Because they can't go home, because their wives won't have them, because they don't have jobs. Yes. *Yes*," he insisted, to Sarah's incredulous stare.

Sarah finally responded. "So my father's responsible for that man, is he?" she asked, cocking her head toward the most hunched-over man at the bar, her voice sounding incredibly clipped and haughty, even to her own ears.

Nick looked like a cat about to lay its claw into a mouse. "Yes, he is," he said softly. "And when you understand that, you'll be more than a pretty smile and a two-hundred-pound sweater," he said, dismissing Sarah and her new outfit with a thrust of his chin.

Sarah felt tears rise to her eyes and threaten to spill over. Absurdly, all she could keep thinking was that the sweater had actually cost seven hundred pounds, not two hundred—and how much that fact would confirm everything Nick had been accusing her and her family of.

Blindly Sarah rose and groped for the door. What seemed like hours later, she found herself finally outside, blinking at what was still daylight.

Two women loaded down with shopping bags passed and looked at her strangely. "Are you all right, miss?" one finally asked, looking like she didn't want to hear the answer to the question.

Sarah shook her head and began to stagger toward the school. It was only a couple of blocks away, wasn't it? Around her Sarah saw that people hung out of the windows, shouting to one another—people of every stripe and color—and that garbage fairly lined the streets. *Why haven't I ever been here before?* Sarah thought. *It's only a couple of blocks from school, but I've never been here.* It seemed strange to her that people should have been eating, drinking, shopping—living life—right near where she had practically grown up and that she should have had no inkling of any of it. *Maybe Nick is right,* Sarah thought miserably, feeling like she'd swallowed a lump of coal.

Someone jerked her around from behind, and Sarah screamed—not a big scream, but a loud one. Chatter stopped on the street for a moment, and Sarah stopped screaming. It was Nick.

"Sarah, love, I'm sorry," Nick said, looking as miserable as Sarah felt.

A man with slicked-back hair in a ratty leather jacket stopped and peered intensely at Sarah. " 'Ee bothering you, miss?" he asked, his accent ringing as clearly as Nick's had moments before.

Sarah forced herself to look at him. Ooh, he was horrid, with his terrible slicked-back hair and threadbare clothes, but she felt a strange comfort in his presence. He was a good man, who would have helped her if Nick truly had been bothering her, Sarah was sure. Somehow this helped her relax—this neighborhood wasn't dangerous; it was only different.

"No, sir, I know him," Sarah said carefully.

"All right, then," the man said, giving Nick a suspicious glance.

"She's my girlfriend," Nick finally explained.

" 'At don't make no difference," the man said sagely, then continued down the street.

They both laughed, and that broke the tension. "He's right, you know," Nick said. "I had no right to talk to you that way—no right at all. Please let me explain it to you so you'll be able to forgive me," Nick pleaded.

Sarah had already forgiven him—the plaintive look on his face had utterly won her over—but she didn't think it wise to let Nick know that, necessarily. "All right," she said, trying to sound as suspicious as the greebly man had.

Nick laughed in relief and took her hand. They began to walk toward the school.

"It was stupid, really," Nick started off, "but I've been nervous about this day ever since we planned it."

"Nervous?" Sarah asked, genuinely confused. How could anything be more nerve-racking than losing one's virginity? *Especially,* she thought, *going to an ordinary pub.* "Why?" she asked.

Nick laughed. "Well, when my father was still around, he used to go to that pub, and so did all his mates," he said. "We used to wait around outside or come in and get them once our mums had sent us in."

Sarah still didn't understand, but she had an inkling that if she remained silent, Nick would have an easier time telling her.

Nick's voice began to take on a touch of the anger he'd displayed in the bar. "There we'd be, dragging home our dads, who were drunk as lords, usually," he said bitterly. "Then Mum would scream at him for the money for a couple of hours, while he just sat there with his hand over his face—or tried to throw a punch in her direction," he added, laughing as if he knew it wasn't funny at all.

Sarah could feel the terrible sadness in Nick—like a yawning pit of black. "I see," she said, although she didn't see at all.

"I'd always thought that the minute you saw where I came from, you'd take one look and you'd want to run," Nick said. "Then I saw you were trying to be so nice about that bar, and I guess I got mad. You weren't going to run," Nick burst out, "so I figured, if you wouldn't tell me what a sodding bum I was, I'd tell you what a stuck-up priss you were," he said, smiling, and squeezed her hand.

Sarah laughed and pressed her head against Nick's shoulder. "I know I don't know anything about the working class or anything," she said—eliciting a snort from Nick, to which she replied with a light slap—"but I want to know. I want you to tell me about the world that I don't know anything about so I'm not just a spoiled little snit."

Nick clasped her hand and turned her toward him. "Sarah, you were never a spoiled little snit," he said. "Just like I'm not a bum like my father—although I was an awful creep tonight," he added hastily.

Sarah buried her head in his jacket. This was the Nick she loved—sensitive, intelligent, kind. "Just as long as both of us remember that," she said, hiding her smile in the zipper of his coat.

Elizabeth wanted to ask Max more about Lavinia, but she was too frightened—if she pressed him about anything personal, he might run. Or tell her to keep her place. Whatever his reaction, Elizabeth wanted to avoid eliciting it.

"What's this?" Max asked, picking something up off the ground.

Elizabeth looked at what was in his hand and gasped. She'd forgotten she'd had a photograph of the Wakefield siblings tucked into her journal. It must have fallen out earlier.

"So this is your sister and brother?" Max asked,

gazing at the photo.

Elizabeth nodded, unwilling to look at her sister's face. "Yes, it's me, my twin, Jessica, and my older brother, Steven."

Max nodded as if he'd finally cracked some difficult math theorem. "Elizabeth, can I ask you something?" he said gently.

Elizabeth wanted to laugh since he'd asked her so much already. "Fire away," she said, eliciting another "I love your American idioms!" from Max.

Max's face turned serious. "I'm so jealous of you—you had all that freedom at university: living with who you liked, studying what interested you, pursuing your writing without difficulty," Max said, his eyes shining as Elizabeth continued thinking of exactly what nightmares all that freedom could reap. "How could you leave?" he finished.

As Max put the question to her directly, Elizabeth realized she had no intention of answering it with the same glibness. The gears in her brain spun as she tried to think of a nimble way to change the subject. "I wasn't at home," she finally offered. "Like you are with Lavinia."

Max looked disappointed with her answer. "Well, when one is not at home, it's important to find it," he said, looking like he didn't quite buy her answer— or something disturbing had occurred to him.

"Speaking of which, I should get back inside,"

Elizabeth said, even though she was dying to ask him more questions about Lavinia. The chemistry between her and Max was too intense for that somehow—Elizabeth felt that like the face of the sun, if she stared straight into it, it would blind her.

Max nodded, looking distracted and cheerless. "Speak to you later," he said.

Had he really meant it? Elizabeth wondered as she descended back into the kitchen, preparing to begin the nightly round of duties that always followed her late afternoon break. An old movie line occurred to her, and she wished she'd used it the minute Max had approached her:

Max, she would have said, fading into a black-and-white swirl, like cigarette smoke, *we've got to stop meeting like this.*

Sarah burped, demurely trying to conceal it behind her hand. Fenwick didn't seem to notice—if he had, he didn't flinch.

The evening, which had begun so awfully, had ended wonderfully—Nick had walked her to the school, then waited in the shadow of the rose-bushes with her for Fenwick to show up. When he arrived at the appointed hour, Sarah had kissed Nick quickly, murmured, "See you tomorrow," and dashed out before he could say anything scary about condoms again.

"Did you find the books you needed, miss?" Fenwick had asked as she'd tossed her near empty satchel into the back of the car.

Sarah flinched. Did Fenwick suspect something? He couldn't. Anyway, he always greeted her with some neutral remark. "Oh, I put them back in my cubby at school," she said, trying to sound breezy. "They're too heavy to lug around everywhere."

She leaned back against the rich leather cushions, her head swimming from all that had happened. Now that Nick had confessed all the fears of his childhood, she felt even closer to him. And all he'd told her! It was like being at the center of some dark, dramatic novel.

Perhaps I'll tell him about Mum, Sarah thought, wondering how the tragedies of her life would stack up against those of Nick's. *Hopefully he won't think that I'm just some poor little rich girl trying to compare my life to his.* She looked out the window at the dark treetops speeding by.

Because I'm not, she added.

Chapter Eight

Vanessa waited until Elizabeth and Alice were breathing slowly and evenly before she felt safe enough to throw off the stiff, chintzy blankets Mary doled out for the servants and make her way downstairs to find the photograph of her mother and the earl.

Why didn't you just take it earlier today, you coward? she berated herself, feeling exposed and ridiculous as she tried to noiselessly descend the main staircase—the second time she had taken it that day. *People who have first- and second-class staircases deserve what's coming to them,* Vanessa thought, thinking of the disarray she would make of the earl's tidy little ordered world the minute she sprang her secret on him.

As Vanessa reached the main foyer, the enormous grandfather clock—which ceased actually bonging the hours from twelve to six in the morning—switched from two fifty-nine to three in the morning with a hiss and whir. Vanessa looked at it accusingly, as if, cartoonlike, she feared that the clock would suddenly reveal two large arms, pin her to its steel face, lift her kicking off the ground, and prevent her from stealing the photo.

"Sod off," she muttered, hastily skipping across the marbled floor toward the wing that housed the earl's study. She halted with a gasp, seeing a figure approaching from the main dining room. Had she been found out? Was that Mary snooping around, damn it all? Was it all over?

Vanessa darted back behind the door, then slowly peeked out again. Just as slowly, the intruder peeked back at her.

Vanessa swiped her hair with her hand. The intruder did the same.

You idiot! Vanessa said to herself, feeling the leftover adrenaline race around her veins like so many scurrying mice. There was no other person—it was just her reflection in the large, gilt-edged mirror across the room that she walked by every day.

Vanessa, get to the earl's study and get that photograph. Stop fooling around.

As calmly as she was able to, Vanessa walked through the hall toward the wing that housed the earl's study. She stopped trying to remain quiet—in this huge house, with its thick stone walls and six-inch doors, if anyone could hear her without being five feet away, it would be a miracle.

And if she did run into someone, she would just tell them that she had heard them—assuming that said person didn't walk in on her while she was ransacking the earl's desk.

Vanessa crossed the passageway and checked under the study's door to make sure that the earl wasn't savoring some tome while puffing away on his pipe late into the night—she had never found evidence of such wee-hour exercises, but you never knew. The door was as black as the vault to an Egyptian tomb.

Breathing slowly to keep herself calm, Vanessa placed her hand on the doorknob and turned it. The hardware was well-oiled by Mary and the rest of the household staff—it barely creaked.

There was no moonlight. Vanessa waited a moment until her eyes adjusted to the dark. The dark study looked like a graveyard, all the old shapes of furniture popping up like tombstones.

Why does everything keep looking like graveyards to me? Vanessa thought with irritation. *You'd think I'd been watching a bloody Boris Karloff film marathon or something.*

Shaking off her fretful thoughts, Vanessa made

her way over to the desk—which she could have found in her sleep, she'd cleaned the room so many times. She debated turning on the light, then decided against it. Although the earl's office was fairly isolated, you never knew who might be awake or who might be awoken by the reflection of the light on the glass. *Good thinking, Vanessa,* she congratulated herself, with more than a dash of sarcasm. *If you hadn't been the indigent daughter of a staggering old drunk, you could have made a great sneak thief.*

Vanessa dropped to her knees and pulled open the drawer she had opened earlier that day. She plunged her hand in, and her stomach fell.

The drawer was empty.

At first Vanessa thought that her eyes must be fooling her—it was a trick of the darkness. But then she swept her hand slowly from one end to the other. Nope. The drawer was empty.

Vanessa felt sick. What did this mean? Could the earl have somehow discovered that she had been nosing around? Was she to be fired tomorrow?

Don't be silly, you idiot, Vanessa told herself. *You've just opened the wrong drawer, that's all. This is one of the empty ones you looked through today. Don't be batty.*

But Vanessa knew it was the right drawer.

Still, she began to open the other drawers,

heedless of keeping them neat, as she had been careful to do earlier. She swept her hand through pens, note cards, envelopes. She triumphantly grabbed a small cardboard box, then opened it to see in the dim light that it was only filled with rubber bands. She had to restrain herself from letting out a cry of dismay and regret.

Dammit, Vanessa, now you've done it. The earl saw that someone messed with his photographs. He must have had some clue—some invisible way—of seeing that they had been looked over. And now he's hidden them again, and you'll never find them.

Vanessa dropped back on the rough Persian carpet, wondering whether to laugh bitterly or descend into a fit of weeping. So close. So close.

You couldn't just slip the photo into your pocket earlier, could you? That would have been too hard, you idiot. And now you've lost the one piece of proof you had. The one piece of proof that would have let the world know what a piece of scum the earl is— and who you really are.

But Vanessa hadn't gotten this far without becoming used to disappointment—her life was almost entirely made up of disappointments as of yet. Her more practical side began to coach her— gently, firmly—not to give up.

Listen. The earl probably moves these photographs frequently. Maybe he was struck by a fit of sentiment and wanted to look at pictures of little Max and stupid Sarah. Maybe he knows that this box contains the photograph that could do him in, so he always moves it every Friday to a new hiding place. Maybe he's given it to Mary to get them all put in some new fancy album.

Vanessa stood, wondering whether it was worthwhile to give another quick search of the office while she had the privacy. She looked around at the darkness and decided against it.

It's extremely unlikely that the earl knows I was snooping—he has no idea who I am, remember? That's the whole point. So he moved them. Who cares? You'll just have to find them again—and make sure you take the photo for yourself this time.

Vanessa felt her breath coming faster and harder—like an animal, panting, closing in for the kill. She shut her eyes. *I was so close, I could taste it,* she thought.

Saturday morning, five minutes after Alice, Vanessa, and Elizabeth had eaten their customary breakfast—tea, toast, and cornflakes with decidedly un-American creamy milk—Elizabeth had already decided it would be easier to build a new house than to clean Pennington House as fanatically as Mary seemed to want it done.

Standing like a drill sergeant, Mary had already

dispatched Alice with the full-length duster and Vanessa with a basket of lemon oil and rags. Now she was explaining to Elizabeth how she was to steam iron all the napkins and tablecloths that were to be displayed for the dinner that night.

Elizabeth eyed the pile with resignation. *If it weren't for Max,* she realized reluctantly, *I would take this evening's torture as an excellent opportunity to quit.*

Listening to Mary chatter about how there was nothing "finer than a proper English table," Elizabeth had another realization. *It's not because of Max that I won't quit,* she thought. *It's because I am deathly curious about seeing the woman he wants to marry.*

After Mary had set Elizabeth up with the old steam press and a fancy smaller iron "for the fine points," as Mary had put it, Elizabeth took the opportunity to sit on the heap of fine linens for a moment, her head aching—both at the thought of such a large amount of labor so early in the morning and at her conversation yesterday with Max.

Oh, why did I let myself get dragged into that huge chat session? Elizabeth moaned inwardly. *It just made me feel like I have some secret, true connection with Max—when the only connection I really have is that I'm going to have to iron the napkin that his fiancée is going to use to mop up her dirty crumbs.*

Elizabeth sighed, rising to her feet. Regret wasn't going to help her get through the pile—and if there was anything she had learned from the Sam-and-Jessica debacle, it was that hard work could sometimes be *really* helpful in taking your mind off things you didn't want to think about.

But the monotony of laying out heavy sections of cloth under the steam presser, then going over the edges with the iron, only encouraged Elizabeth's mind to wander back to their conversation yesterday. Not only had Max seemed so interested in her life—*which* is *kind of interesting right now,* Elizabeth thought, *if you find mopping floors interesting*—he had taken the first step toward explaining why he was definitely going to marry Lavinia—*and why I,* Elizabeth thought, *am definitely delusional about thinking there's a chance that anything could happen between us, ever.*

"But what would happen if you just didn't marry Lavinia? If you just worked on your novel, like you want to, and let someone else take your father's position in Parliament?" Elizabeth had finally asked—quaking inwardly all the time that Max might discern that she was asking the question out of more than idle curiosity.

Max had blanched, and a strange look had crossed his face—as if Elizabeth had asked him why he hadn't tried eating raw liver every day for a

176

year. "That wouldn't—that just wouldn't—do," Max finally explained.

But Elizabeth, her old journalist roots kicking in, had pressed further. "Wouldn't do for who?" she had asked. "For your father or for you?"

Again a look of distaste had flitted across Max's face. "In England we're not as—as *self-directed* as you Americans," he had said, forming the term in such a way that Elizabeth could be sure it wasn't entirely complimentary. "My responsibility to my family—to my family's name and to this house—is *part* of me," he said. "Giving it up would be like giving up an arm or a leg."

But wouldn't you gain something in the process? Elizabeth had wanted to say then but hadn't.

Wincing now at how pushy she must have seemed, Elizabeth felt the same despair she had felt at how different she and Max really were. The fact of the matter was, the whole idea of allegiance to a title and a family seemed as goofy and foreign to her as an episode of *Fawlty Towers*. But to Max, Elizabeth had to admit, it was more than a concept—his responsibility was very real, and the roots ran deep. If he broke off from his family, Max seemed to be saying, like an uprooted tree, he would simply wither into the dust.

Elizabeth shivered, now ironing napkins with such a steely efficiency that the pile to her left had tripled in size. *Well, I'm not like that,* she thought. *I'm an American girl, and I can't help it. I think people should pursue their own dreams—not the dreams of their family.*

Especially if that family thought up those dreams practically five hundred years ago, she added.

Mary popped her head in, and Elizabeth started, scared that she was about to be disciplined again—argh. "Ah, Elizabeth! You're almost done. When you finish, come help Vanessa with the dusting." Mary disappeared just as quickly.

Elizabeth shook her head, then began to laugh at the imitation of Mary with which Vanessa had regaled her and Alice last night. "Now, *guhllllz,*" Vanessa had said, stretching out the word as Mary did when she was doing her rendition of a high-class accent. "If you will simply follow the duchess around with a broom and dustpan *at all times,* I'm sure we can avoid the types of accidents we witnessed last year *with Lord Ashbery. . . .*"

Lord Ashbery, Elizabeth had divined, was a distant, five-year-old cousin who had wreaked havoc in the earl's study on a visit last year.

Alice had played the dutiful maid. "Oh, yes, miss! No worries, miss! May I be so honored as to dump the crumbs from milady's plate into the waste bin as well, miss?"

Vanessa had fixed Alice with Mary's hawklike

stare. "No, miss, you may not. That is an honor reserved"—here Vanessa had paused to take a haughty breath—"for myself."

Last night the girls had all dissolved into giggles—glad for one moment to be free of the tyranny of their lowly positions at Pennington House. A moment later Mary had knocked angrily on the door, then entered. "There is entirely too much noise here!" she had declared, looking at all of them as if she'd like to eat them alive. Vanessa had assumed a look of such fervent obeisance that Elizabeth and Alice had had to struggle not to burst out laughing in Mary's face. When she had finally left, they had descended on their beds, biting their pillows to keep Mary from hearing their laughter out in the hall.

But now Elizabeth could feel the familiar knot of tension gathering again—a tension that probably, after seeing the famous duchess, would only increase.

Elizabeth tossed the last napkin on the heap and slammed the steamer shut.

It was going to be a long day.

Sarah rose with the early afternoon light slanting through the blinds, looked over at her bedside clock, then lay back with a sigh of pleasure. *Who cares if it's nearly three o'clock?* Sarah thought. *Nick loves me, anywhere and anytime.*

Well, Nick hadn't exactly gone that far. But Sarah could tell from the way he had acted—and from the way he kissed her.

Sarah rolled over into her warm sheets, determined to savor all the events of the evening once more before showering and beginning her day. Now that the date was over, she decided, she didn't even regret how horribly it had started. If Nick hadn't behaved so abominably, Sarah was realizing, she wouldn't have had a chance to be so magnanimous with him when he'd tried to make up.

And wasn't it just brilliant how he chased me all that way? Sarah thought. *If I had run into the Tube, I'll bet he would have still chased me down there too—however far I went.*

Knowing that Nick was desperate to keep her gave Sarah a delicious feeling—a feeling that all but removed the stain of violence Nick's earlier anger had spread over the evening. *Well, he was sad,* Sarah thought. *And worried. It was just like the explosion you get when you open a bag of crisps—one bang and it's all over.*

But Sarah couldn't help the feeling of disquiet that crept over her whenever she thought of how beastly Nick had really been. She tried to shake it off, not wanting a hint of unease to pollute the warm feeling she'd felt when they'd clasped hands and walked back to the school.

There was a knock at the door. "Come in," Sarah called sleepily, hoping desperately that it wasn't her father. It wouldn't be, though—her father liked to have conversations mostly on his own turf—not when Sarah was lolling about in bed and half asleep.

Max entered, looking a bit sheepish. "Feeling better?" he asked gently.

For a moment Sarah thought Max was being sarcastic. A sharp retort was on the tip of her tongue when, luckily, she remembered that the last time Max had seen her, she had been at death's door. "Much better," she said happily, trying to look satisfactorily "cured," curling up into a ball and smiling at her brother.

Max looked relieved. "Good. I was worried we wouldn't have you for dinner tonight!" he said, with what Sarah could tell was an absurdly false heartiness.

Sarah almost gave a groan of dismay—she had forgotten that tonight was that appalling dinner with the duchess and her bloody boring aunt and uncle. Ugh! Hours at that infernally long table in the large dining room with a bunch of adults who were about as fascinating as a saltshaker and a bowl of blood pudding. If only she could have remembered to play sick, then sneaked out to Nick's during the feast!

"Oh, yes—La-*vin*-ia," Sarah teased. "Wouldn't miss it for the world."

"Lovely," Max said, and turned to leave. He turned back. "Would you like a cup of tea or something?" he asked politely.

Dear brother, I know you're quaking in your boots about marrying someone you couldn't give less of a fig about, Sarah wanted to say, *but you could show a little genuine brotherly concern, you know? Some compassion. I'm not only someone to take the heat off you—I'm your sister. What if I really were sick?*

"No," Sarah said. "I'll be up and about in a bit."

But Sarah had no intention of drawing any attention to herself—the way to handle this evening, she had already decided, was to flirt with James like mad, keep Elizabeth in Lavinia's face—and Max's—the entire evening, then sneak out once maximum crowd cover was reached.

But Max—dear, stodgy Max—wasn't going to be allowed to catch wind of any of her plans. She would play the perfect sister—as much as she could without arousing his or anyone else's suspicions, of course.

"Max," she said honestly, stretching her toes out as far as they could go, "I wouldn't miss tonight for all the world."

Chapter Nine

Max had spent the entire day wandering around in a fit of anxiety. First he had attempted to practice his cricket swing out in the back, by the old tables. He hadn't been able to hit the ball at all—not one swing. Then he had attempted to work on his thesis, but he had found himself instead at the Web sites of his favorite literary magazines—looking at the prizes and contests being offered with a mixture of longing and guilt. Finally he had roused Sarah— his sick sister!—just to alleviate his own stress. Relieved that she wasn't still unwell, Max had made sure to establish that Sarah was definitely coming to the dinner that evening.

For some reason, he felt sure that he couldn't tolerate it without her.

Well, without Sarah you'll be left with your father, Lavinia, and her aunt and uncle, Max thought.

Not a pretty picture, is it? I mean, there's James, after all—but he'll be too busy mooning over Vanessa, as usual, to help me out.

Max tried to calm himself down. *It'll be different when it's my and Lavinia's house—our house— and our parties,* Max thought. *When we're united before the world, I won't feel so much that she's my enemy.*

I hope, he had added miserably.

But now it was six o'clock—the appointed hour—and Max had managed to stuff himself into a smart black suit and a blue shirt Lavinia had gotten him on a recent trip to Italy. *That will make her happy,* he thought, inanely unable to dismiss the masochistically logical thought that followed. *But what have I done to make her unhappy?* Max wondered. *And why do I know she must be?*

Sarah had appeared—uncharacteristically—on time, and she was dressed in a smart black sheath skirt, with a fetching red sweater. Her cheeks glowed as she brought the earl—looking his usual self—a drink and sat on the edge of his chair and chatted. *Sarah's getting old,* Max suddenly realized, the vision of his sister speaking with his father far more affecting than the talk with the earl about her "morals" had been. *She's growing up into a beautiful young lady, and I'm getting married. By next Christmas, I'll be an old married man.*

The chimes rang, and Max turned toward the door. *So why do I feel like I'm just going through the motions?* he thought desperately.

He heard the murmur of Mary and Lavinia's voices, and then Lavinia swept in, followed by her aunt and uncle. "Hello, Max," Lavinia said coolly, placing her hand on his arm while she kissed him dutifully on the cheek.

As usual, Max found himself completely, ineluctably overwhelmed by Lavinia's beauty. Normally she toned her incredible gorgeousness down on a daily basis by pulling back her hair and wearing very plain, deceptively expensive clothing. Tonight, however, she was simply ravishing. Her hair was swept back on either side with bone clips, and the rest tumbled, golden and straight, down her back. Diamonds glittered at her ears. She was dressed in an exquisite ice blue silk gown, which pulled in tightly to her extremely small waist, then swept down to the floor. Glittering shoes peeked out from beneath the hem.

"Lord, you look lovely," Max said, meaning it completely. *You,* he told himself, *must be an idiot not to be head over heels in love with this girl.*

Lavinia turned toward him and gave him a warm smile. "You're very handsome yourself," she said, and a wave of her perfume hit him. *Perhaps I am a little in love at that,* he thought, feeling dizzy at his proximity to this exquisite creature.

Max took a huge gulp of wine. "Drink?" he asked Lavinia.

While he was off getting a glass of the very excellent dry white wine that his father had fetched especially from the cellar for the evening, James arrived. Max handed Lavinia her drink, fetched James a drink, and then installed him at Lavinia's side—*the better to chat up the in-laws,* Max thought.

And could you be any more the picture of the dutiful, loving fiancé, Max? he asked himself sardonically. *Better slow down on the wine.*

Max chatted with Lavinia's aunt and uncle—perfectly nice people who liked him and his family very much—while the earl took Lavinia's arm and engaged her in a deep conversation. Sarah flitted between all the groups, spreading the occasional glee of adolescence on the staid and adult gathering, and James stood in the corner, trying not to peek out of the corner of his eyes for Vanessa. Max totally sympathized. *Thank God for Sarah,* he thought, more than once.

Finally they sat for dinner. Max had hardly been able to take his eyes away from Lavinia, but that changed when Elizabeth entered, hefting a tray of salad plates, followed by Vanessa, who carried the plate of greens and silver tongs.

"We're delighted that the wedding and reception will be held at good old Pennington House," Lavinia's uncle boomed in Max's general direction.

Max took a moment to answer, distracted by Elizabeth's circumnavigation of the table. As soon as he realized the comment had been directed at him, he jerked himself back into the conversation, hoping desperately that no one had noticed what—or *who*—had distracted him.

"Yes, yes," Max responded, trying to smile. "That's what Lavinia wants, after all, and I defer to her in all these matters."

Lavinia fixed a cool smile on Max. "Wise, wise!" Lavinia's uncle boomed, slapping his leg and raising his water glass toward Max in agreement. His wife gave Max a stiff smile.

But Max was struck by the tableau of Elizabeth serving salad over Lavinia's shoulder. Elizabeth was dressed in a variant of their normal uniform—black pants instead of khaki and a white oxford shirt—and her hair was pulled back. Her face looked flushed, as if she had been working very hard for hours—which she probably had, Max reflected. Still, it was astonishing: Elizabeth was every bit as beautiful as Lavinia—*more so*, Max thought, clutching his water glass fervently. *Oh, Lord, am I in a fix here.*

Sensing his gaze, Elizabeth caught his eye

briefly, then looked away as if his look had burned her. Max's eyes shifted, and he found Vanessa's eyes boring, catlike, into his own.

The earl raised his glass—oblivious as ever, Max hoped. "A toast to the newlyweds," he said.

They all raised their glasses, Max's most firmly. He smiled broadly at Lavinia, then at James, then at the earl and at Sarah—to reassure them that *no, no,* he was not gone on the little scullery maid, not at all.

Lavinia didn't smile back, and Sarah cocked an all-seeing eyebrow.

The dinner had begun.

Lavinia had fulfilled every nightmare Elizabeth had ever had about "the other woman." At least with Jessica and Sam, Elizabeth had known that Sam couldn't have been attracted to Jessica because she was better looking. *Better dressed, maybe,* Elizabeth thought, *but for all other purposes, identical.*

But this Lavinia was another story. *I'm sure no one would even be* allowed *to be her twin,* Elizabeth thought sarcastically. When she had entered the dining room with the first course, she had actually almost drawn back, as if she had been dealt a physical blow. *I mean, I heard Lavinia was pretty,* Elizabeth thought, *but this is too much.*

Elizabeth had had all sorts of ideas about how Max's fiancée might look—ideas that she had pretended not to entertain until she was forced to, faced with the truth. One fantasy had Lavinia pegged as a true English rose: a kind of spindly blond with a turned-up nose and saucerlike blue eyes. Or, Elizabeth thought, she might have been the gawky younger sister of an English rose: tall, gooselike, and awkward, like some of the English women she had seen about, whose resemblance to the quacking breeds of the avian nation was more than passing. Elizabeth's favorite fantasy, however, involved a Lavinia that strongly resembled Camilla Parker-Bowles in her youth—horsey, broad, entirely unenviable.

But Lavinia was none of those things. She was, in fact, their complete opposite. *Just my luck,* Elizabeth thought miserably. Dressed in a silvery gown, her neck banded with what must be a real diamond choker, Lavinia could have been a model. *No, she's too pretty to be a model!* Elizabeth amended. *What she looks like—what she actually is—is a real-life princess, straight out of the fancy illustrations in a book of* Grimms' Fairy Tales.

Suddenly finding herself feeling very self-conscious about her sweaty face and straggly ponytail, Elizabeth had assiduously avoided the eyes of anyone around the table while she served the salad—exactly as the earl would like her to behave, she thought, bristling at the thought. Once she'd glanced up briefly and been shocked to find Max looking back at her. She had cast her eyes down in shame. She had to stop seeming like such a stalker—she was only the maid, after all!

"From the left. From the *left*," Vanessa hissed as Elizabeth hesitated over Lavinia's glossy shoulder.

Elizabeth prayed that she wouldn't send an artichoke heart tumbling down Lavinia's expensive—and impressive—décolletage. *She doesn't even know you're here*, Elizabeth thought unhappily. *She's been served by people exactly like you for her entire life, and you don't register any more in her consciousness than the doorknob or the tablecloth.*

Then Elizabeth's all-American pride kicked in. *No, she hasn't*, Elizabeth thought. *She's never been served by Elizabeth Wakefield, and if you plunked her in the middle of Sweet Valley, California, all her titles and diamonds wouldn't mean squat.*

Elizabeth dropped three olives on Lavinia's plate. *Although her* looks *would*, Elizabeth added thoughtfully. *And truthfully, the diamonds and titles probably wouldn't hurt either. I mean, look at Fergie. Except that Fergie pushes Weight Watchers. But Lavinia would never need to do that*, she added, glancing at Lavinia's perfectly trim figure, trying to cut off her bizarre train of thought before it reached epic proportions.

"Are you all right?" Vanessa asked as they

reached the kitchen, having doled out the salad without incident, Elizabeth was glad to realize.

Elizabeth tried to snap out of her stupor. "Of course! Why?" she chirped, putting on the California-cheerleader smile that was practically her birthright, even though she had never used it before, to her knowledge.

Vanessa pointed to her hand, then gently disentangled her fingers from around the salad tongs. "You were holding that like you wanted to disembowel somebody with it," she said, more gently than she usually spoke, especially to Elizabeth.

Elizabeth smiled bitterly. *No one but myself,* she thought.

Vanessa began to load a platter with sliced beef, popping a small piece in her mouth after looking around quickly for Mary. "Don't let the bastards get you down," she said, hoisting the tray over her shoulder and disappearing through the swinging kitchen door.

Elizabeth immediately felt a little better. *I mean, girl, shmirl,* she thought. *That thing out there is superhuman. I can't compete with that. And there's no reason I should think that I have to. I've had plenty of boyfriends, but Max and Lavinia—all these people—might as well be from outer space for all they share with me and my life. So I'm going to go out there and serve them their entrée, and I'm not going to give it another thought.*

Elizabeth picked up the soup tureen and moved toward the swinging door.

Except she knew she would.

Sarah felt like she was actually going to *careen over* with boredom. *Next stop, soup,* she thought, focusing her gaze on the puddle of orange nuclear waste Cook had dreamed up that still lay untouched in her bowl.

First, the assembled party had discussed the wedding for nearly eighteen hours—all through hors d'oeuvres and into the salad course. What kind of music Max and Lavinia would have, how her father and her mother had had Scottish bagpipes at their wedding, how Lavinia's deathly boring aunt and uncle had had a quartet play Mozart all through their own ceremony. Then the adults had moved on to a discussion of flowers, and Sarah thought she would never hear the end of zinnias, dahlias, gladiolas, and roses. What were they going to discuss next—the brand of toilet paper Pennington House would stock its toilets with?

I wouldn't put it past them, Sarah thought. *And anyway, it would be a nice change of pace from this agony.*

Then the assorted company had spent another nineteen hours talking about hunting. It seemed that Lavinia's uncle had ridden over every rock and stone in England, and he was perfectly contented to wax on about every pheasant he'd ever flushed out from behind a bush since he was eight years old. *Old man, if you don't stuff it, I'm going to pluck off your feathers and spit on you!* Sarah wanted to shout into the livery old windbag's face.

Looking across the table, Sarah noticed that Max looked like he was experiencing an entirely distinct order of agony from Sarah's, and she looked on her brother with sympathy. *That doesn't mean I'm not going to go ahead with my plans, though, Maxie dear,* she thought, wanting to kick him under the table just to break the monotony.

Finally Sarah was forced to turn to James and begin flirting much more avidly than she'd planned, just to make sure that she didn't head off to the land of Nod before the main course was even served. She was in a fine mood for it, though—she'd been stealing sips from his claret through the entire meal, banking on the fact that he was much too distracted by Vanessa's comings and goings to notice.

"You know, we're studying economics in school this term," she piped up, tearing James away from the one ear he held cocked to Lavinia's uncle's ramblings.

"Is that so?" James answered, fixing on her a bright, impersonal smile. *You idiot—how dare you condescend to me,* Sarah thought with fury. *I'm going to make you wish you had eaten a bowl of dirt for dinner instead of coming here.* Outwardly she merely smiled back. "Oh, yes. We're studying the European Union," she chirped up.

James immediately went into professorial mode. "Well, that's actually fascinating," he began, as if it were beyond Sarah's powers to normally discuss anything remotely interesting to him. "Are you looking into the Euro?" he asked, then plunged into a minilecture Sarah was sure he had delivered many times. *But that doesn't mean you have to deliver it to me, you hideous windbag. I have a boyfriend, you know, and he never babbles on like you,* she thought, taking comfort that she could think nasty things even if she couldn't say them. "Because the implications of a unified monetary system actually stretch far beyond Europe's borders . . . ," James went on, not noticing that Sarah's eyes had become distinctly glassy.

Sarah wanted to toss a glass of ice water straight into his pompous, babbling mouth, but that wasn't part of her plan, unfortunately. She'd have to stay polite to put that into motion. Out of the corner of her eye she could see that the earl was watching them fixedly. She was sure that he was nearly splitting his sides with joy that Sarah—his wayward daughter—had finally chosen an *acceptable* crush. *Thank God it's working,* Sarah thought. *There's no way I could stand it if it weren't.*

"Oh, no, I'm much more interested in France," Sarah broke in, opening her eyes very wide—innocence was key!—and moving in closer to her prey. Her knee brushed James's, and he looked slightly alarmed, to Sarah's great amusement.

"France?" James said, struggling with his wineglass as if it were a sticky car door. Finally he managed to gulp down the remaining drops that Sarah had left untouched. He looked at the glass with confusion, and Sarah had to restrain a giggle—James must think his wine had spontaneously evaporated.

"The implications," Sarah said, letting her voice grow very low and husky, "of the Euro in France."

James nearly overturned his water glass, then managed to deliver it to his mouth without spilling. He put it down carefully, then pushed back his chair, trying to disguise his withdrawal in a stretch. "Is that right?" he asked, hiding his discomfort with an unconvincing facade of friendly interest.

As if I'd ever really *like you, you conceited pig!* Sarah wanted to shout. But instead she moved closer—it was terribly fun to flirt with a man in whom you weren't interested in the least, she was realizing, because there was no risk, and you could wreak havoc willy-nilly. *Unlike with Nick,* Sarah thought, trying to kick away the feeling of slight panic she still associated with him ever since last night—and with thoughts of the night to come.

"Yes," Sarah said, and dropped her voice even lower so that James was forced to come even closer to hear her at all. "The implications of the Euro on . . . relations," she nearly whispered.

James looked like he might dissolve into a puddle of ooze. "Relations?" he whispered back, then coughed. "Relations?" he said normally.

Sarah flipped her hair over her shoulder and gazed at him coyly. "Between . . . men and women," she said, leaning over quickly for her water glass and draining it completely. *Catch any cleavage, James?* she thought. *Not that I have any to speak of.*

Sarah put down the glass, fearful that if she looked at James, she would burst out laughing. She could feel his terror, but she knew that he would stay polite at all costs—that's how these boys were raised, after all. *Not like Nick,* she suddenly thought. *Is that why I like Nick? Because he's nothing like these stodgy, pasteboard boys?*

"Well," James said, leaning back again and coughing aggressively, "I think that might be rather more of a sociological question than an economic one. There are statistics on marriage and whatnot that one can obtain. . . ."

Sarah immediately tuned him out, smiling and nodding at intervals while gazing at the traffic around the table. As usual, Lavinia looked like an ice sculpture—*one I'd like to crack into a thousand pieces,* Sarah thought. *That would be a real improvement over her current personality.*

James was unable to stop looking at Vanessa every time she came into the room, Sarah noticed, giving off such waves of longing that she was surprised it didn't knock the maid over. And Max was no better—each time Elizabeth ran through with a plate of something, he jerked around like a rabbit—trying so aggressively to *not* peek at her that he seemed like a reverse compass, swinging away in tandem wherever Elizabeth turned. And the earl, it seemed, was in love with the duchess's aunt and uncle—being convivial with his wine and joining them in shooting triumphant glances at the "happy couple."

In a few hours you'll be part of your own happy couple, Sarah thought, then suddenly choked on her sip of water. In a few hours she would be with Nick. Losing her virginity. And she'd only barely snogged him!

"Are you all right?" James asked vaguely, giving Sarah a hearty whack on the shoulder that seemed rougher than was strictly necessary.

"I'm fine," Sarah sputtered, taking James's hand off her shoulder and returning it to his lap. Forget flirting—this was serious business. This was the real, adult world, and there was no backing out now—not if she ever wanted to see Nick again.

"I'm fine," Sarah lied, hiding her agony under a big, fake grin that she bestowed on the table at large. Her father raised his glass in greeting across the table, and Sarah raised hers back. "Something just went down the wrong way, that's all," she lied.

Chapter
Ten

James was incredibly relieved when dinner finally ended and the leftovers from dessert were pooled on sticky plates. Sarah had been flirting with him the entire evening—up against his leg, even!—but now she was gone, having drifted off upstairs with some vague excuse about a tummy ache. God— the terrors of adolescence—James was glad he was out of it. Not that adulthood was any better, mind. Vanessa had entered and reentered many times, like some beautiful, sightless ghost, keeping her eyes firmly on the opposing wall and away from James, as far as he could see, at all times. Now she was nowhere to be seen. The other maid—the blond one—had circled the table already three times with coffee for the still chattering earl and Lavinia's aunt and uncle.

"Want to go upstairs to see my computer?"

Max suddenly turned and asked him, as if they were nine years old and Max had just gotten a new and fabulous toy.

James couldn't think of anything better than leaving the table, where he was practically suffocating for lack of Vanessa sightings. "Yes!" he said, then hoped he hadn't sounded too rudely enthused.

Max rose with an also too obvious enthusiasm. "Just going to show James the new laptop," he declared to the assembled company.

The adults murmured assent while Lavinia looked stone-faced. James noticed that Max avoided looking at her, thinking idly that Max had certainly perked up every time that blond maid—who was quite pretty, in fact—had entered the room.

"Trouble in paradise?" James murmured as they headed upstairs.

Max blushed, then looked down at the polished stairwell. "Don't ask," he muttered tersely.

James made a mental note to ask—definitely— after they had gone over the laptop for some acceptable period of time.

They entered Max's plush digs, and Max propped open the smooth black machine. "See, it doesn't even need a phone line," he bragged, clicking on the icon that dialed up the Internet remotely. "It's cellular, I think," he hazarded. "Maybe satellite."

James ran his hand over the smooth graphite case. It was a beautiful object—enviable, really. But what did that matter if Max still looked as miserable as he had downstairs?

"Max, what's going on?" James asked quietly.

With a sigh Max punched the laptop shut. "What do you mean?" he asked in a high, unnatural voice.

James knew all about Max's avoidance techniques—that manly, high-end reserve in which the earl specialized—and he wasn't having any of it. He decided to lay his cards on the table. "Doesn't have anything to do with that maid downstairs, does it?" James asked, hoping desperately that Max hadn't done anything stupid.

Max had put his head in his hands and was wearily stroking his temples. He looked up, surprised. "Is it that obvious?" he asked, with genuine alarm.

James smiled—so he had been right on the mark about the maid. *Hope you didn't do anything that can't be reversed, my man,* he thought. "Well, you did look like you were living for those moments when she spooned gravy onto your veal," James said carefully.

Max began to mock pull at his hair. "Damn, damn, damn, damn!" he spat out.

"I don't think anyone else noticed," James said hastily.

Max buried his face in his hands again. "Oh, it's hopeless!" he wailed, showing more affect than James had ever seen in him.

This was a delicate situation. "What—er—exactly has happened?" James asked.

Max looked up, his eyes sunken far back in his head, like all the liquid had been sucked out of his body. "Nothing like that, James," he said, sounding deathly serious. "Nothing like that at all."

James felt relieved—at least Max hadn't been tomcatting around on Lavinia—which would have been impolitic, to say the least—and completely unlike Max. So what had been going on? "What exactly happened?" James repeated.

Max pushed the computer away and sat down on his office chair, staring off into space blankly. "Just that I've got a raging crush on Elizabeth Bennet," he finally said.

Although he completely sympathized with Max, James almost burst out laughing at the ludicrousness of their respective situations. Here they were, two scions of the British empire—in line for the throne, practically—completely gone on two scullery maids at the same estate. And here was the kicker—evidently neither of the maids would have them!

James attempted to make light of the situation. He had always envied Max's ability to smoothly accept the responsibilities of his position—not that

Lavinia was so hard to accept—and he couldn't help but feel slightly gleeful over the fact that Max was evidently chafing at the bit just as much as he was.

"Well, now you know what it's like to want someone you can't have," James said, smiling.

Max looked up at James with stormy consternation. "It's not the same at all, mate," Max spat. "At least you could have Vanessa if she would have you. Me—my wife's picked out for me. My life's picked out for me. You're free as a bird, but I'm stuck."

Instead of feeling chastened by Max's words, James felt a rising prickle of hope—an anxious, skittering hope. Could what Max had just said be true? Did James simply need to tell Vanessa how he felt about her?

"You don't have a beautiful fiancée waiting to let a pack of wolves loose on you and split your bones for the marrow if you so much as think of another woman," Max said, twirling a pencil aimlessly around on his desk. He stopped himself. "I shouldn't make out that it's Lavinia who's territorial. She's not. She just wouldn't want me in love with another woman, of course, which is perfectly reasonable. But still, James"—Max roused himself—"it's not the same at all."

James tried to control his rising excitement, but Max's words had started a chain of thought he couldn't hold off with his fears. It was true—Max had made promises, set dates. But he, James, had no seat in Parliament waiting for him and no fiancée with a model's face and an account at Harrods. All he had stopping him were a set of expectant parents and his own expectations—and the desires of one beautiful Vanessa, of course. But he would never know what those were unless he confronted her and made it clear that he had no intention of just using her.

"I've been a fool," James said in wonderment, "and a coward. I've got to tell Vanessa exactly how I feel about her and take my lumps with the rest of the men."

Max smiled bleakly. "I wish you luck, mate," he said. "I'm glad one of us has the freedom to take that chance."

James grabbed Max's hand and shook it, then gave him a hasty pounding on the back until he gave Max a wild coughing fit. Then he exited the room, feeling guilty for not bringing Max a glass of water first, heading down the main stairway at lightning speed.

"Have you seen Miss Vanessa?" he asked Mary, who was passing from the dining room toward the kitchen area.

Mary looked back over her shoulder at the scattered platters on the dining table—the earl and company must have retired to the parlor, James thought—then fixed her eyes on James. "I believe she's in the kitchen area, sir," Mary said, "but I'll locate her for you, if you like."

For the first time James didn't blush, demur, or stammer at the offer. "Yes, please, Mary," he said, setting his legs apart and standing firmly, as if he would wait forever if need be. "Many thanks."

For the longest minute he had ever spent, James stood watching the corridor that led from the kitchen to the dining area. Then Vanessa—looking like a black-haired angel, James thought—appeared.

"Yes?" Vanessa answered, her lovely face, as usual, remote and utterly impenetrable.

You can hide if you like, James thought, staring at her blocked-off beauty, *but I won't hide with you anymore. You're going to have to see me, and answer me, whether you like it or not.* "I have something to say," James heard himself say, as if from a great distance. *I seem to have left my body,* he thought, looking down at his hands and worsted-wool suit sleeves as if they belonged to someone else.

For a moment James thought Vanessa's eyes gave off a flicker of anger. The flame immediately cooled, however, and they returned to that same black emptiness, like ash left in a grate.

"As you may be aware, I have had feelings for you for a great deal of time," James began, immediately wincing at his formality. *Calm down, mate, it's not a doctoral defense,* he cautioned himself. He tried to soften his words. "I like you, Vanessa," he said, trying to pinpoint the center of that endless black in her eyes—the part that would lead him to *her. Look at me!* he wanted to command, and he had to stop himself from grabbing her arm or taking her hand in his, so great was his intensity.

"Vanessa," James said, swallowing at his temerity—was he truly going to come out and say it? "Is there any chance you have feelings for me?"

Vanessa stood stock-still for a moment, looking off at a distant wall. Then she darted out of the room like a rabbit.

James had prepared himself for a slap, a hearty laugh, even—in his most hopeful of fantasies—a passionate kiss. But the only reaction he hadn't prepared himself for was—none at all.

James's entire gut ached. *Why, I'm right back where I started!* he thought. *No—worse. I'm behind where I started.*

No—now I know that Vanessa hates me for sure, James realized, not even able to laugh.

Elizabeth had left off stacking endless plates in the enormous dishwasher to bring cognac and coffee to the assembled guests since Vanessa was, in Mary's words, "nowhere to be found." "And soon to be unemployed," Mary had snapped with great irritation as Elizabeth wished fervently that she possessed Vanessa's knack for ducking out during the most tedious portions of anything.

"May I refill your glass?" Elizabeth asked Lavinia's aunt politely, sneaking a glance at the still beautiful Lavinia, who was seated on a small love seat with the earl. The aunt smiled widely, holding up her cognac glass, and Elizabeth dutifully took it.

"See here, girl," Lavinia's uncle commanded. Elizabeth jumped—it had been a while since anyone had called her "girl," if they ever had. "Bring me a scotch and soda, will you? And make it damn quick," he added, turning to clip his cigar.

Charming, Elizabeth thought, heading over to the bar to mix drinks. She decided to stop at the love seat on the way out, however, and pause until she was noticed, as Mary had rigorously drilled into her that she must. *It's part of my job, after all,* Elizabeth thought, trying not to smirk. "Yes, Elizabeth?" the earl finally asked.

"May I offer his lordship or her ladyship anything?" Elizabeth asked the two, trying her best not to make eye contact with either of them.

Lavinia yawned. "No," she said, as if Elizabeth had offered her an old beaten-up shoe.

"No, Elizabeth. That will be all," said the earl.

God, does this man ever say anything else? Elizabeth thought.

Elizabeth walked from the room, her face burning. As she stood over the bar mixing the scotch and soda, she heard the earl's booming laugh, followed by a series of genteel whinnies that could only have come from Lavinia. As silly as Elizabeth knew she was being, she couldn't help feeling that they must be laughing at her.

No. They don't even see you, Elizabeth, she thought, feeling that she'd like to bury her head in the ice bucket. *For people to laugh at you, they have to notice you.*

Although she had left America specifically to *avoid* seeing certain people—*people who will remain nameless,* Elizabeth thought, squashing thoughts of Jessica and Sam violently—Elizabeth suddenly realized that she had never thought that cutting all her ties in America might create a situation in which no one would see *her* either. *If I'd been at the writing program, things would have gone differently,* Elizabeth thought sadly. *I would have had teachers, colleagues, friends.* Elizabeth saw herself walking through a Tudor courtyard with a gang of boys in suits, like an extra in *Dead Poets Society. Here, if I get a "Well done" from Mary or a "That will be all" from the earl, it's a red-letter day, conversationwise.*

Suddenly a geyser of rage rose up in Elizabeth. In the other room the earl was chatting affectionately with Lavinia, a well-educated, beautiful, charming girl. *Well, I'm a well-educated, beautiful, charming girl too,* Elizabeth thought indignantly, her irritation providing one of the few instances in which she felt justified in acknowledging her good looks. *The only difference between us is that her people colonized millions and gave themselves a lot of silly titles. Is that something to be proud of?*

Angrily uncorking a new bottle of cognac, Elizabeth answered her own question. *Well, it's exactly the reason our founding fathers left this idiotic country,* she inwardly seethed. *For an American it's nothing to be proud of at all.*

Slightly amused at how her envy of Lavinia had prompted a sudden attack of patriotism, Elizabeth's rage cooled. She smiled and was preparing to head back into the parlor when she heard someone speaking to her.

"He'd only use you, you know," a voice hissed behind her.

Elizabeth turned, scarcely believing her eyes and ears. There stood Lavinia, looking at Elizabeth like she was a specimen under a microscope. And *seeing* her too, to be sure, Elizabeth thought, suddenly regretting her wish to be noticed. No happy invisibility here.

"Oh, you're pretty enough, I'll grant you that," Lavinia continued, her perfect reflection looking as smooth and cold as marble to Elizabeth in the lamplight. "But you mustn't take Max's wedding jitters for anything more than they are—nothing. He enjoys looking at pretty girls, that's all. So whatever you're planning—whatever you're *hoping*," Lavinia sneered, "just put it out of your mind right now."

Lavinia's high-toned inflection cut into Elizabeth's self-possession like a razor. However, the fact that Lavinia was talking to her also gave her a boost of confidence. See—she was very visible indeed!

Elizabeth wouldn't have predicted that she would have faced a showdown like this so calmly, but her amazement at Lavinia's bold confrontation, she decided later— plus having dealt with a crazy sister for so many years—gave her the strength to give back as good as she got.

"I'm afraid I have no idea what you're talking about," Elizabeth said, lifting a cognac glass in one hand and the scotch and soda in the other. She moved toward the door, then turned around toward the line of gleaming bottles. Lavinia's eyes had narrowed to positive slits, but Elizabeth faced them without fear.

"There's fresh ice in the bucket," Elizabeth said. "I'm sure you know what you can do with it."

*   *   *

Sarah was triumphant. After she had flirted with James for at least an hour, the earl had gone from mild happiness to complete joy. After an hour and a half, he had felt confident enough, Sarah saw, to turn to Lavinia's aunt and uncle and talk about partridges—*he's already seen our engagement, wedding, and first child being born,* Sarah thought happily as she sneaked upstairs.

After throwing on some jeans and a sexy V-necked top, Sarah brushed out her hair and applied some gingery lipstick. Blotting her lips, she looked at herself in the mirror. *All right, dearie,* she told herself, making sure her bra straps weren't peeking out. *Bombs away.*

After throwing some overnight things in a bag and calling a cab in a hushed tone, Sarah walked gingerly down the front steps. All the dinner-party goers, as she'd hoped, were tucked away in the parlor, and none of the household staff were anywhere about. After taking a deep breath, Sarah opened the front door and walked out into the cool night.

Now, don't worry. You'll just go over there and see what's what, Sarah thought, skipping down the long drive toward the empty country road. She shivered.

In less than five minutes the cab was there. "Thank God," Sarah muttered to herself. So far, so good.

"Good evening," the cabdriver said as Sarah got in. She gave him Nick's address, then settled back, reaching into her bag for a pack of stale cigarettes she had filched off Victoria a couple of weeks ago. She pulled one out and stuck it between her lips, rummaging around for a pack of matches. She'd practically turned her purse inside out when she looked up with dismay. She smiled. The driver had already clicked his lighter and was holding the flame backward for her.

Sarah felt a little thrill run down her spine. So this was what it felt like to be an older woman. *A far cry from Fenwick,* she thought, feeling like a girl in a movie as she leaned forward to light the tip of her cigarette. "Thanks," she said, catching the driver's eye. He was a Sikh, his turban brilliant white in the darkness. She leaned back to puff on her cigarette with satisfaction as she watched the scenery change from outskirts to city through the windows.

Before Sarah knew it, they were sitting in front of Nick's. Sarah hesitated, then pulled some pound notes out of her bag.

"Thanks," she said to the driver.

"Good night, miss," the driver said. "I'll watch you get in."

"Oh, thank you," Sarah said, feeling a little lost as she left the cab. *What's wrong with me?* she thought.

As she stepped onto the walk, she realized what

she had been waiting for. *Why, I was waiting for that driver to give me permission to go!* she thought.

Or to tell me not to, she added.

Trying to stop her legs from shaking, Sarah waved the cabbie off, mounted the steps to Nick's house, then rang the bell.

Before, it seemed, her finger had even left the ringer, Nick was standing there. "Love," he said, enfolding her in his arms. He leaned back and looked at her, smiling and shaking his head. Sarah had to fight the urge to pull out of his embrace.

"What?" she finally asked, disliking the idea of being looked at with such intensity. *I don't look that good,* she thought with irritation, surprising herself—since, of course, she normally liked to think that she *did* look that good.

Nick's smile grew even broader. "It's just that you look so beautiful," he said, his hand settling onto the small of her back. Sarah shivered—was it from thrill or fear? *Or is it just cold?* Sarah mocked herself.

Slowly Nick led them up the stairs to his bedroom. *What's wrong with me?* Sarah thought, barely able to focus on the cheap, tattered furniture, the dusty carpeting, the piles of rubbish in every room. She felt like this was all happening to another girl, in some movie or TV show. *I'm supposed to feel all excited, like I can barely wait for Nick to kiss me, even touch me. But instead I don't feel anything.*

Nick opened the door to his bedroom. "Home sweet home," he said, dimming the lights immediately.

Sarah didn't know what to say. A plaid comforter lay half stretched over an unmade bed. A heap of beer cans had evidently once been a pyramid, but it had clearly tumbled down a long time ago. The brown, tufty carpet looked like some fungus that had grown over the floorboards for the last twenty years.

"It's . . . nice," she finally managed.

Nick laughed, popping a beer can and taking a large gulp. "Not quite Buckingham Palace, is it, Lady Pennington?" he said, and burped.

Sarah stiffened. *It doesn't need to be Buckingham Palace,* she wanted to say. *But you could have made the bed, at least.*

As if he had read her mind, Nick walked over to the bed and sat on it, patting the place beside him. "C'mon, little Sarah," he crooned. "Time for bed."

Perhaps Nick was going to be nice now, like he was at school, Sarah hoped. She walked gingerly over to the bed and sat down beside him, trying not to let her extreme discomfort show in her face. This would all end soon, she thought, and Nick would become the boy he had been at school—romantic, slightly aloof, his hard edge making him dangerously cute to a girl with a protective father.

Nick leaned in for a kiss, and Sarah tried not to

recoil from his beery breath. He pressed in anyway, his tongue feeling like a flummoxed slug in her mouth. *It's never felt like this before!* Sarah thought. *Where's the Nick I've been kissing this whole time?* "How much have you had to drink?" Sarah finally gasped when Nick came up for air.

Nick seemed unruffled. "A few," he said, stroking her neck. "Why, would you like one?"

No, Sarah thought. *I'd just like you to brush your teeth!*

"No," Sarah said. "This just isn't . . . exactly like I pictured it."

The minute she said it, she knew she'd made a tactical error. Now it was Nick who drew back, his eyes narrowing. "Oh, it isn't, is it?" he asked, sneering. "What did the Lady Pennington expect? Six footmen and a bower of roses?"

The fact that Nick kept accusing her of being snobbish was starting to get on Sarah's nerves—especially when *she* was offering *him* her virginity. *If I wanted Wills, I'd be dating Wills, wouldn't I?* Sarah wanted to scream. *But I'm dating you. And it's not like we're just going out for an ice cream cone!*

Sarah's temper rose. "No," she said. "But it wouldn't have hurt if you'd bothered to make the bed!"

Nick's face clouded over, then became suddenly dazed with teenage lust, as it always did when they were kissing at school. "Why make the bed," Nick asked slowly, looking into her eyes, "when we're just going to unmake it?"

Before she knew it, Sarah found herself on her back, touching the icky, unwashed covers, with Nick on top of her. He was really heavy, Sarah realized—she could barely breathe. "Now, just relax," Nick said insistently, stroking her thigh. "Just relax and let me do everything."

Sarah felt like she was being squashed to death. "Nick, no!" she heard herself saying, as if she wasn't even in her body anymore. "I'm not—I'm not ready yet!"

Still Nick kept pressing Sarah back onto the bed, even though she was fighting to get free as hard as she could. Was he just going to ignore her? Was he going to treat her like she wasn't even there? *This is a monster,* Sarah thought, trying to squirm away from his mouth. *This isn't Nick at all.* "Everyone's nervous the first time," he said, kissing her neck. His hand moved up her thigh. "Just relax, baby. Relax."

Baby? Sarah thought. A moment later she found herself standing at the door, with Nick glowering on the bed, holding his chin in his hand in disbelief.

"You stupid twit," he said, looking from the blood on his hand to Sarah, then back to his hand. "What'd you do that for?"

Sarah looked at the fresh scratch marks on Nick's chin, wanting to burst into tears. "Nick, I'm sorry," she began, faltering, although not wanting to move any closer to the bed again. "I didn't mean to—"

"You're damn right you're sorry!" Nick thundered, coming closer. He grabbed her wrist, twisting it upward. "I'll make you sorry!"

Pain shot through Sarah's wrist as Nick forced her toward the bed. "Nick!" Sarah began to scream. "Stop it!"

"You dumb bunny," Nick said. "Looking down your nose at me!"

That did it. Sarah brought her other arm around and jabbed her fingers in Nick's eye. He yelped in pain, dropping her wrist. Sarah bolted from the room and down the stairs, only stopping to grab her purse off the floor.

"Sarah!" she heard Nick call as she flew out the front door. "Sarah!" he yelled, holding the front door open into the night as she ran out onto the sidewalk.

Sarah ran for a couple of blocks—she wasn't sure how long—until she was sure Nick wasn't following her. *Of course he's not following you, Sarah,* she told herself. *You scratched half his face off.* Panting, she felt tears starting in her eyes. Where was she anyway? And how could she get out of here?

Well, that was a success, Sarah thought miserably,

trying to get her bearings. This was supposed to have been her great romantic outing, her first foray into adulthood. Instead it had just been a mess—a bigger mess than anything Lavinia and Max were getting into by getting married, even if they didn't really love each other, Sarah was forced to admit.

Holding her wrist tightly so it didn't jounce against her side, Sarah started looking around for a cab. Seeing one parked just at the opposite corner, Sarah hailed it, got inside, and gave the driver directions to Pennington House. "Are you all right, miss?" the driver asked, looking at her in the rearview mirror.

Sarah fumbled in her purse for a compact and looked at herself in the tiny mirror. Even in the dark of the cab she could see that her mascara was running, her hair was in disarray, and her lips looked like someone had tried to crush them like two cloves of garlic.

Wiping under her eyes and raking her fingers through her hair, Sarah tried to make herself look vaguely presentable. "I'm all right," she called to the front, hoping that would satisfy the driver.

Except I'm not, she thought.

The more Sarah thought about it, the more she felt like she should have seen this side of Nick from the beginning. She had never held his past against him—she had tried to understand it and had felt like it didn't matter who his parents were or where he came from. And it really didn't—in fact, it made it more exciting. But what basically mattered was Nick.

But he never did the same for me, Sarah thought dejectedly. *All the while I must have been just this big joke to him, this big conquest. Lady Pennington this! Lady Pennington that!* Tears rolled down her cheeks. *And he was just going to use Lady Pennington to get even with anything bad that ever happened to him in his life.*

The betrayal was too great to bear. She had really loved him—or thought she had—and now . . . this. Unable to control herself, Sarah put her face in her hands and sobbed.

"Miss," she heard the driver saying. "Miss!"

Sarah lifted her head. They were sitting outside the gates of Pennington House.

Sarah opened her purse, but the driver put up a big, meaty hand. "On the house," he said. "Not that you need it." He jerked his head toward the large house in the distance. "But still, miss, it seems that you do need it, like."

Sarah had to restrain herself from opening the front door and throwing her arms around the neck of whatever stranger sat there. "Thank you," she finally said, almost unable to get out the words.

In the darkness Sarah could almost feel the driver

grinning. "No worries," he said, and sped off, back toward London.

Left in the silence of Pennington's grounds, Sarah could hear her own breath—harsh, ragged. She stood in the moonlight, wiping the tears off her face with her sleeve.

On the way up to the house she chucked Victoria's cigarettes into the woods.

Chapter Eleven

"Max, I know," Lavinia was saying.

They were in Max's car, speeding away from the Thurstons', having just dropped Lavinia's aunt and uncle off at home after the long dinner. The statement hung in the air like a glimmering bubble—one Max was loath to burst and destroy.

"What do you mean?" he finally asked cautiously.

Lavinia sighed heavily, snapping her beaded purse open with a click. She took out a compact and opened it, checking her face in the moonlight. "You and that girl," she snapped. "That maid."

Max had a visceral desire to sink into the ground—to actually *drive* himself underground, as if his car were a submarine. He had to shake himself into attention to keep his eyes on the road. "What in the world are you talking about?" he finally asked, careful to enunciate each word calmly.

She's just being crazy, he thought. *She saw Elizabeth, and she's jealous. Throw her off the scent.*

Lavinia turned toward him, and Max winced, worried she was actually going to strike him. But it was only her words that were violent. "Oh, Max, don't be stupid!" Lavinia spat. "You and that maid," she added, drawing the words out malevolently. "You *like* her, Max."

Max tried to look confused—and innocent. "Lavinia, I don't know what you're talking about," he said, his voice taking on an angry edge. *Be firm with her,* Max thought. *Be firm, and she'll give this up.*

Lavinia flung her purse against the windshield, and Max almost braked. "Lavinia, don't be childish!" he shouted. "You almost made me get into an accident!"

Lavinia laughed, but without mirth. "Oh, do shut up, Max," she said, and was silent for a moment.

Thank God, Max thought, hoping the storm was over.

When Lavinia spoke again, her voice was menacing. "Don't you dare ever shout at me again, Max," she said. "It's you who's getting me in an accident. It's you who has a crush on some stupid maid. And if you marry me when you're in love with someone else, I shan't ever forgive you."

Max laughed. Somehow he had become fake

man, and he couldn't come back from it. "Well, I should hope not!" he joked.

Lavinia turned and flung the full force of her words on him—Max could feel each drive into his skin, like little spikes. "Max, don't you dare lie to me!" she exploded.

Max quickly pulled the car over to the side of the road and turned off the engine, looking straight ahead while the car ticked and settled. Beside him he could feel Lavinia breathing heavily, like a caged tiger.

Max traced the wheel with his finger. "Lavinia, you are being ridiculous," he finally said. "There is nothing between me and anybody."

Lavinia gave a harsh laugh. "Well, that's certainly true," she said.

Max began to grow frustrated. "Dammit, Lavinia," he shouted. "We're getting married, aren't we?"

Lavinia was looking sullenly in the other direction. Her voice was different than any tone he had ever heard. "I don't know, Max," she said. "Are we?"

Max had to fight the urge to step out of the car and slam the door, just to get some space. "Of course we are," he said icily. "We picked the invitations out just last week."

Now Lavinia turned to look at him. "No, Max," she said. "*I* picked the invitations." She began to breathe deeply, as if she was trying to stay in control. "You had to work on your never-ending thesis. Remember?" she said, choking back a dry little cough.

A thousand protests rose in Max's mind—about his work, his career, his thesis due date!—but they all died on his lips. *She's right,* he thought. *Why am I torturing her? Why am I trying to get her to believe something neither of us believes?*

"Lavinia," he began. "I—"

But Lavinia had gathered a fresh round of anger. "Just tell me," she hissed. "Just look in my face and tell me that you are not attracted to her, and I'll stop."

Max felt himself grow cold—it seemed he could see himself and Lavinia very far below and then the roof of his car. He reached very deep inside to find his voice.

"I'm taking you home," Max said.

Lavinia sat back and said nothing. They sped down the road toward her estate. When he glanced her way, he could see that her cheek was completely dry.

Finally he pulled the car to a stop in front of her door. "I'll call you tomorrow," he said, and walked around to open the door for her. She had already walked out herself, however, and was at the door, looking into her purse. Max ran to catch up with her.

"Good night, Lavinia," Max said earnestly, reaching for her elbow. She jerked away, refusing to look at him, simply pulling her key out of her clutch. Max dove for her cheek, but she turned to the side, opened the door, and went inside, like he wasn't there at all.

Max stood on the doorstep, feeling insanely guilty. *Tell me what to do!* he thought at no one. *I can't cut her loose, but I don't think I can give her what she wants either!*

Driving back toward Pennington House, Max realized there was a cruel irony in Lavinia's pretending that he wasn't there. *Well, I'm not really there, for her,* he thought. *Am I?*

As he pulled up to the house, he was startled to see a girl—disheveled, clearly crying—walking toward the entrance. He jumped out of the car and ran toward her.

"Sarah!" he said, turning her around to face him. "Is everything all right?"

For a moment Sarah looked at him like she didn't recognize him. Then her face broke into an angry look of contempt.

"You just live in your own private castle world!" Sarah screamed. "You don't know anything about my problems or anyone else's, for that matter. Go to hell!"

Max stood there, stunned, as Sarah, sobbing, ran

into the house and slammed the door behind her.

Well, that's two women who've slammed the door in my face tonight, Max thought. *Will someone make it three?*

Suddenly the back of Max's scalp prickled. He looked up toward the large picture windows on the servants' floor, and there stood Elizabeth, like a ghost, looking down on him, clearly having just witnessed his scene with Sarah.

Max wanted nothing more than to run up there to her—to confess all his troubles, to talk to her about Sarah, to talk to her about *everything*. *If anyone could help me now, it's Elizabeth,* he thought, feeling like even more of a jerk for betraying Lavinia yet again.

But he couldn't even raise his hand in greeting. Max was locked to the driveway. Locked by all the distance—and promises to others—that still separated them.

Max jerked his head down in shame. *Why can't you talk to her, man?* he asked himself. *Why can't you talk to any of them? Just choose. Just be a man and choose. Stop torturing everyone—especially yourself.*

Max jerked his head up again to try to meet Elizabeth's gaze.

But the window was empty.

*   *   *

Sarah burst into her room, heedless of waking the earl or even Mary, who was always snooping about. Flinging herself full length on her bed, she began to sob as if her life depended on it.

When she finally arose from her stupor, she didn't know if hours had passed or merely minutes. Turning over in the bed to blow her nose, her eye caught the album that she had cast aside the other day.

Once again Sarah began to turn the aging pages. Each page brought on a fresh round of tears. *What did I do wrong, Mother?* Sarah thought, weeping. *He seemed too good to be true, and I guess he was. Still, I wish you were here to tell me what to do. I wish you were here so we could eat ice cream and you could tell me what a jerk he was.*

Sarah came to the last page, to a large photo of her mother taken shortly before her death. Her mother gazed toward the camera as if she held some secret—some secret that, Sarah was sure, could make everything all right if she just knew the answer.

I wish you were here, Sarah thought again, closing the album for good.

After Elizabeth left the scene with Lavinia, she had briefly celebrated in the kitchen, hurling plates and cups into the dishwasher with uncharacteristic abandon.

"You're certainly happy to be washing dishes tonight," Alice had remarked.

"Oh, I'm just glad this dinner's over," Elizabeth replied in a deliberately even tone.

"Amen to that," Alice said.

But inside, Elizabeth felt briefly triumphant. If Lavinia was angry, Max must have some feelings toward her, right? Lavinia didn't seem like the kind of girl to get her feathers ruffled easily.

So it wasn't all my imagination, Elizabeth thought joyfully, up to her elbows in suds. *Max and I do have this—connection.*

It was only when Elizabeth went upstairs—totally filthy, her shirt sodden—that the entire truth had struck her. And her sudden happiness escaped like the air seeping out of a balloon.

Why, it doesn't really matter if Max likes me back, Elizabeth realized, *if he doesn't do anything about it.*

A low moan escaped her, and she sat on her cot, glad that Alice and Vanessa had not yet come to bed. *Where are they?* she wondered idly. *What is it that they find to do around here? What kind of personal lives do they have?*

I'm sure any of it's realer than my dumb fantasies, Elizabeth thought.

Because she had *always* known, Elizabeth realized, on some level, that Max liked her, of course. That connection was undeniable. But the fact that it was shared by the both of them to the extent that it could be recognized by others (like Lavinia) didn't take away the fact that Elizabeth was a maid and Max had a fiancée. And a job in Parliament waiting for him. An entire house that had been in the family for generations. Which all equaled an entire life planned out, with no room for one Elizabeth Wakefield.

Elizabeth wanted to smack herself on the forehead for being so dumb as to let herself get caught up in a silly fantasy. A dumb, silly fantasy that some man on an island thousands of miles away from her home was going to take her away from . . . all the problems at home.

I'm just running, Elizabeth thought. *I'm just running away from my problems as fast as I can. And I want to use Max as my getaway car.*

Suddenly she was distracted by shouting outside. It sounded like a girl was screaming at someone—was Alice or Vanessa in trouble? Elizabeth turned and walked quickly to the window, pulling aside the curtain.

Below stood Max and a young girl. It took Elizabeth a minute to recognize her as Sarah, she looked so furious and disheveled. Sarah was screaming at Max, and Max was just standing there. Suddenly Sarah let out one final string of abuse, turned on her heel, and ran into the house.

Elizabeth could practically feel the door slam through the floorboards.

Then Max looked up.

His eyes passed through Elizabeth like a lightning jolt. With a cry she stood back and dropped the curtain.

He's not just a getaway car, Elizabeth thought. *It's something else—something more now. But everything's too mixed up inside to figure it out.*

It took all her courage to go back to the window. *I'll just look at him,* Elizabeth thought. *Forget about Sam and Jess. I'm here now, and I have to deal with it.*

Elizabeth took a deep breath and closed her eyes. *Okay. No more running. I'll just try to make some kind of contact, and then . . . we'll see.*

She pulled the curtain aside and opened her eyes.

But Max was gone.

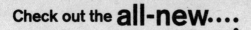